NANCY WARREN

RIBBING AND RUNES

VAMPIRE KNITTING CLUB
BOOK THIRTEEN

Ribbing and Runes, Vampire Knitting Club Book 13, Copyright © 2021 by Nancy Warren

Cover Design by Lou Harper of Cover Affairs

All rights reserved.

No part of this book may be reproduced in any form or by any electronic or mechanical means, including information storage and retrieval systems, without written permission from the author, except for the use of brief quotations in a book review.

Thank you for respecting the author's work.

ISBN: ebook 978-1-990210-09-9

ISBN: print 978-1-990210-08-2

Ambleside Publishing

INTRODUCTION

Can a secret runic message lead to murder?

As Lucy and Rafe plan their wedding, everyone wants to get involved. The vampire knitting club are crafting the gown, William's catering, the Miss Watts are making the cake. Everything's under control. Or is it? Just as Lucy begins to believe there won't be a hitch in their plans, she receives a curious wedding gift that leads to murder.

Between hen parties, her parents arriving early, running a knitting shop and a murder, will Lucy make it down the aisle in one piece?

Get the origin story of Rafe, the gorgeous, sexy vampire in *The Vampire Knitting Club* series, for free when you join Nancy's no-spam newsletter at NancyWarrenAuthor.com.

Come join Nancy in her private Facebook group where we talk about books, knitting, pets and life.
www.facebook.com/groups/NancyWarrenKnitwits

PRAISE FOR THE VAMPIRE KNITTING CLUB
SERIES

"THE VAMPIRE KNITTING CLUB is a delightful paranormal cozy mystery perfectly set in a knitting shop in Oxford, England. With intrepid, late blooming, amateur sleuth, Lucy Swift, and a cast of truly unforgettable characters, this mystery delivers all the goods. It's clever and funny, with plot twists galore and one very savvy cat! I highly recommend this sparkling addition to the cozy mystery genre."

— JENN MCKINLAY, NYT BESTSELLING
AUTHOR

"I'm a total addict to this series." *****

"Fresh, smart and funny" *****

RIBBING AND RUNES

CHAPTER 1

 lanning a wedding is stressful at the best of times, but when the groom is a vampire who's been around for more than half a millennium, the guest list gets complicated. However, Rafe and I had easily agreed that we wanted to keep the number of guests to a reasonable limit. We'd probably have opted for a low-key registry wedding if it hadn't been for my mother. We'd visited my parents in Egypt to tell them the good news in person, and to my surprise, my archaeologist mother, who spent her life in chinos, work boots, and a field hat, went all mother-of-the-bride on me.

"Oh, how I've dreamed of this day," she'd said, misty-eyed. "My baby, finally getting married."

What was this "finally" business? I wasn't even thirty yet.

After that we traveled to New Zealand, where Rafe had a collection of rare manuscripts to evaluate, and we took some time to enjoy each other away from the prying eyes and busybodies who surrounded us at home. It was fantastic, and in three weeks of sightseeing and relaxing, of being treated like the most important woman in the world, I was more than ever certain I was doing the right thing. Because marrying a vampire comes with some issues, let's face it.

We arrived back in Oxford to find the members of the vampire knitting club were determined to knit or crochet my wedding dress, and William Thresher, Rafe's butler and general manager of the estate, was already planning menus. Needless to say, a simple registry office wedding was pretty quickly off the table. We agreed to hold the wedding at Rafe's manor house, which would soon be my home, too, and I started buying bridal magazines.

I asked my cousin Violet to be a bridesmaid. Our friend Alice agreed to be the matron of honor. Jennifer, my best friend from Boston, was coming, as we'd been promising to be each other's bridesmaids since we'd watched *Friends* together as kids. Lochlan Balfour, Rafe's friend from Ireland, would stand up for Rafe.

William would cater the event, and his sister Olivia was doing our flowers. The whole event was falling into place so easily, I got nervous.

So far, so good. Then came my trickiest dilemma.

What was I going to do about Gran? She was a vampire but too recently turned to appear in public. But how could I not invite my beloved grandmother to my wedding?

It was a problem I couldn't solve, and it was Gran herself who came up with the solution. "My love," she said when I asked her what to do, "I can watch your wedding from the window."

There were so many rooms with windows in the estate that it would be simple to arrange the ceremony so Gran had a perfect view. I hugged her. "It won't be the same as having you right there, but it's a brilliant idea."

"I'll be right beside you in spirit, as you know," she replied.

We didn't put an announcement in the local paper or anything, as we wanted a private affair, but somehow word got out. To my delight, congratulations-on-your-engagement cards started arriving at the shop and Rafe's home, as well as a few gifts.

I think it would be fair to say that wedding fever gripped the vampire knitting club the minute they found out that Rafe and I were getting married.

I was excited, too. Who wouldn't be? I was marrying the love of my life and soon to be moving into what Rafe called a manor house and I would have called a castle, and, to be blunt, my money worries would be over. He was also brilliant, entertaining, occasionally funny, and a vampire. I appreciated that no relationship was perfect, but getting past the undead thing had been the biggest sticking point to us finally getting together.

But now that I'd made the decision and had the emerald and diamond engagement ring on my finger to prove it, the vampires were all in.

There'd been some initial fear that I might give up Cardinal Woolsey's Knitting and Yarn Shop when I got married, but as soon as I reassured them that I wasn't quitting my job, all worries were at an end.

They had opinions on everything. Where we should honeymoon, whether I should keep the flat above the shop in case I ever needed to stay over in town, and even whether Nyx would be happier staying with them when I went home at night. Nyx was my black cat familiar. I appreciated that they were willing to let her stay in the labyrinthine tunnels underneath Oxford where some of the vampires had their lair, but I assured them that Nyx would be perfectly fine commuting along with me. She was my familiar, after all.

But perhaps the most excited conversations were around what I was going to wear.

It became pretty quickly apparent that I wasn't going to go to a bridal boutique and pick a dress. The vampire knitting club fully intended to make my wedding gown. I'd never even known you could knit a wedding dress, but they showed me pictures of knitted and crocheted dresses that were absolutely gorgeous.

I tended towards something with a higher neck, but Sylvia kept edging me toward something off the shoulder and low-cut.

We were standing in my back room, where I ran classes and the vampire knitting club met. Sylvia, Gran, Clara, and Mabel had come in through the back way with more dress patterns. I was a little nervous, as only a curtain separated the back from the front of the shop, and I didn't want to risk Gran being seen. It tended to upset customers when they discovered the supposedly dead former proprietor of the shop wandering around.

However, there were no customers, and I kept an ear tuned for the bell so I could scurry out front if anyone came in. Violet was supposed to be serving in the shop, but she was on her tea break, and who knew when that would end?

Sylvia showed me yet another hand-knitted gown with a plunging neckline. I finally said, "I don't want anything low-cut."

Sylvia glanced at Gran and then at me, her gaze going to

my cleavage. "It's so much more practical, dear. For later." She looked at me significantly.

I'd never seen a look of embarrassment on Sylvia's face, and I wasn't positive I saw one now, but she definitely looked a little odd. Gran was looking down at the floor as though searching for dust bunnies.

"For after what?" I had no idea what these two were on about.

"The wedding night," she said, finally.

I still wasn't getting it. "What's my neckline got to do with my wedding night?"

I knew these two were old-fashioned, but they'd been born at the end of the nineteenth century, not the seventeenth.

Finally, Sylvia almost shrieked, "For when he turns you."

I was so stunned, I stood there in silence for a second. "Turns me?"

"Into one of us," she said at last.

I took a step backward. I didn't mean to; it was instinct. "You think Rafe is going to turn me into a vampire on our wedding night?"

"Yes," she said, as though I were being thick. "It's the logical thing to do. As part of the ceremony."

"Not any wedding ceremony I want to be part of."

I looked at my grandmother, and she finally lifted her gaze to mine. I wasn't positive, but I thought she appeared relieved. Sylvia not so much. I tried to explain my position. "It's not like we haven't talked about it, and I love Rafe. You know I do. But I don't want to be a vampire."

I didn't want to hurt their feelings, but I liked food way too much and preferred to look in the mirror to put on my own makeup. Maybe I was looking at things through too human a perspective, but I didn't want to have to worry about the sun any more than a fair-skinned person with concerns about the ozone layer would.

"But then you'll leave him all alone," Clara said. She was sentimental and inclined to state the obvious.

I nodded. It was, I admitted, the great sadness of my approaching nuptials. "I know. But he still wants to marry me, and he's the one with the most to lose." It would be great for me. I'd have a man who had the looks and strength of a thirty-five-year-old for my whole life. It would get weird as I got older and he didn't, but we'd cross that bridge when we came to it.

Gran took over the conversation then. "Well. Now that we've got that settled, there are more wedding gown choices available to you."

We finally settled on a crocheted gown that would be done with pure silk crochet thread. There were separate lace flowers that could be crocheted individually and then sewn on, as well as a beautiful shawl and a detachable train. This was important, because every single member of the vampire knitting club wanted to know that they had made a piece of my gown, so there had to be a lot of it.

The only difficulty was that Rafe couldn't see the gown before our big day, so we had to have extra meetings in secret. I suspected he knew what was going on, but he was a good sport, and if I told him he couldn't come near or by my shop, he didn't.

"And what about filling the tradition of something old, something new, something borrowed, and something blue?" Mabel asked. Before I could say a word, she eagerly said, "I'd be delighted to lend you something. Something to wear, perhaps."

I had to school my expression to remain calm and not gape at her in horror. I sometimes wore sweaters Mabel had crafted, out of kindness. She was a brilliant knitter but had the worst taste of anyone I'd ever known. The thought of wearing something of hers on my wedding day gave me a thrill of horror.

I was pretty sure everyone else felt the same way. Gran said, "I'm so glad you brought that up, Mabel. I've been wanting to talk to Lucy about my own wedding dress."

We all turned to stare. "You still have your wedding dress?" I asked her. I wasn't fabulous at math, but I thought she'd gotten married around 1960. I lived in her house now. I'd never come across an old wedding dress. I'd have remembered.

She looked a bit superior as she said, "If you'd ever bothered to go up in the attic, you might be surprised what you'd find."

"There's an attic?" I supposed I knew there must be one, but I hadn't really thought about it, and I certainly hadn't spent any time searching. Unless your ceiling leaked or you had vermin, did you ever need to go in the attic?

She said, "There's not much up there. But I did store a few special things. Including my wedding dress."

"But we're going to crochet Lucy her wedding dress," Sylvia said, sounding aggrieved.

Gran nodded. "My dress is too old-fashioned, anyway, but I thought perhaps you might like the veil or the buttons are quite special. We had a very happy and a long marriage, your grandfather and I. It would make me very happy to think of you carrying the tradition forward."

Well, what could I say to that? The poor woman couldn't even attend my ceremony since she'd be outed as a dead woman walking. The least I could do was wear a bit of her dress. Even if I wore the whole thing, it would still look a whole lot better than anything Mabel would come up with.

Gran grew nostalgic. "Sometimes my wedding seems like yesterday. What a happy day that was."

"I bet."

She looked around at all of us. "Shall we go up and look now?"

I had to wait for Violet to return, so Gran suggested that she and the three other vampires go upstairs and open up the attic, and then I could come as soon as my cousin returned.

I didn't want to miss anything. "Don't have any fun without me," I warned them.

She glanced at me, and I supposed she was silently letting me know that I could have gone up to that attic any time since the house had come to me, if I'd been so interested.

They went up to my flat, and Nyx, ever curious, decided to leave her usual snoozing spot in a basket of wool in my front window and follow the vampires upstairs. She was right. It was certainly more exciting up there than it was in the shop. I forced myself to do a quick tidy of the wools.

The door opened. But it wasn't my shop assistant or a customer. It was Theodore, another of the vampires and a great friend of mine. He'd once been a police officer and now ran a small business as a private investigator. He was from the pre-technology era and very thorough in his investigations. If you wanted someone followed discreetly, Theodore was your man. He had a baby face hiding a sharp brain. He was also an artist.

He glanced around to make sure there was no one around and then said, "Lucy, I've an idea for your gift."

Clearly not a surprise present then. "Okay." I probably sounded tentative, having just dealt with Mabel's suggestion that I borrow some of her clothing for the wedding.

He looked rather pleased with himself. "I've just come from the art supply store. Now, I'm not a great artist. But I did criminal sketches in my work with the police."

I wasn't entirely sure what crime had to do with my wedding. Hopefully nothing. He was looking at me as though waiting for me to understand where he was going, and I totally didn't, so I must have looked blank. He went on, "And I paint a lot of the sets for Cardinal College's theater productions."

I nodded. I knew this. I'd even helped at their Midsummer Night's Dream, though it had been more of a nightmare.

"Well, I'm offering you my services as a way of recording your wedding. Since photographs would be incomplete."

I all but banged myself on the forehead with the palm of my hand. How had I never thought about this? When I'd dreamed of my wedding day, I'd imagined photographs would be involved. But I was going to look pretty stupid looking at a wedding album that contained me and what would appear to be an imaginary groom.

I went forward and threw my arms around Theodore. "That is the best gift ever. Thank you so much."

He looked bashful. "Are you certain? We could hire proper portrait painters."

I shook my head. "No. I don't want anything stiff or fancy and formal. I think you'd do a beautiful job. Thank you."

He was so pleased, he said, "I shall begin practicing right away. I may even go to Crosyer manor and sketch in some backgrounds so I can concentrate on the two of you on that happy day." And then he headed with his bag of supplies into my back room, which led via a trapdoor down into the tunnels beneath Oxford and to the apartments beneath.

Violet came in soon after. She glanced around. "Why is it so quiet today?"

I shook my head. "I don't know. Some days are like that, aren't they?"

"Well, perhaps I should leave early." She glanced at me hopefully.

I nipped that idea right in the bud. "I'm needed upstairs. Gran has her old wedding dress she wants me to see. Apparently, it's been tucked away in the attic all these years."

"That's nice," she said, sounding mournful. "My grandmother has her wedding dress all tucked away in tissue, but I doubt I'll ever wear it."

Not only was she taller and larger in scale than her grandmother, but I couldn't imagine she'd want to wear a vintage dress. Violet was more the bohemian type. However, I didn't think she cared what she wore. She wanted to get married. And, based on her experiences ever since I'd arrived in Oxford, her dating record was sketchy at best.

"Have you been back on Witch Date?" I asked her.

She shuddered. "Please, I've learned my lesson. No."

I didn't want to bring up William, Rafe's butler and estate manager, but I was fairly certain she had feelings for him.

Sometimes I thought maybe William had them for her, too, but it was so hard to tell.

As though changing the subject, I asked, "Have you helped William out with any catering gigs lately?"

She rolled her eyes and then went behind the cash desk to put her purse away. "Please. The man's obsessed with your wedding. He thinks of nothing else."

Well, that was good. For me at least.

Impulsively, I reached out and grabbed her hand. "It will happen for you, you know."

She looked up at me sadly. "Will it? Sometimes I think it's this town. If you're not some freakish genius, you don't really fit in in Oxford, do you?"

"Well, I'm no freakish genius. I do okay."

She snorted. "You've got Rafe. And this shop. What do I have?"

"You've got friends. Family. You're part of this shop. You have your witch sisters."

She began to straighten up the magazines. "I just feel restless. That's all. Don't mind me. It'll pass." Then she jutted her chin in the direction of the door leading up to my flat. "You'd better get going. Unless you want unsupervised vampires in your attic."

Immediately, I headed toward the door. "Good point. Bad enough having them in the basement."

Luckily, two customers came in then, so Violet had something to do. I slipped through the door that connected the shop with the stairs up to my flat. I ran lightly up the stairs and found no one in the living room. I stopped and listened. They hadn't waited for me. I ran up the second set of stairs and found them in the guest bedroom.

I'd never paid any attention to the hook in the ceiling all the times I'd stayed here, but it turned out that there was a tool inside the cupboard that hooked onto a metal ring. By pulling it, Gran opened a door in the ceiling that pulled down a ladder that unfolded in sections.

"That's so cool," I said.

"Lucy, dear, you really must get to know this house better," Gran said.

Of course, she could have told me about the entrance to the attic. I suspected she'd forgotten about it, too. She said, "I'll go first. Just in case the floor's rotted away with age." I didn't think she was worried about rotting floors. She was eager to be the first one up there. And, since she'd presumably tucked away whatever was stored up there, it seemed fair she should go first.

Now that Gran was a vampire, she wasn't at all frail, as she had been when an elderly mortal. Her legs were strong and sleek, and she went up that narrow ladder like a twenty-year-old.

"There's a light up here somewhere." Her voice came down to us muffled. There was a rustle and a bang and then, "Ah, here it is." And then, sure enough, an electric light glowed through the attic opening.

"You go next, Lucy," Sylvia said, shooing me forward. I was certain she was dying to get up there too but was being polite. I didn't scamper up as quickly or smoothly as my grandmother had, but I managed. The attic wasn't that large. It had a peaked roof that appeared to be in pretty solid shape to me. It was cool and dry in here, which seemed good. There were boxes, a couple of trunks, some old, broken furniture, and a few old paintings dotted around.

If we stayed in the middle, we could stand.

While the others climbed up behind us, Gran went straight to a dust-covered trunk, unlatched the brass latch and opened it up. She got to her knees, and I joined her, kneeling down beside her. A faint smell of lavender and a smell like wood chips wafted up.

"It's lined with cedar," she said. "It should have kept the moths out."

I felt like a little girl playing dress-up as we looked through the various items in the trunk. There were old photographs, theater programs and menus, old fashion magazines and commemorative newspapers about Queen Elizabeth's coronation.

She sighed over a broken watch. "That was the first gift your grandfather gave me."

The clothing was fun. A velvet coat and an early Chanel suit caught my eye. I imagined I'd come up again when I wasn't jostling for space with nosy vampires.

"Where's the dress?" Sylvia demanded. She was much less interested in Gran's trip down memory lane than I was.

Gran dug down. Her wedding dress was in a linen zip-up bag, carefully folded. She eased it out, and I helped her unzip the bag and remove the garment within. "My wedding dress." Gran held it out on its padded pink silk hanger. The dress was tight-fitted in the bodice and flared out, coming probably to just below her knee. It looked like something Audrey Hepburn would have worn. I was glad Gran wasn't planning to lend me the whole dress, because I did not see myself in this. Instead, she turned it around and showed me the back. At first I thought she was showing me the bow, and then the light shifted and I caught the gleam in the buttons. I leaned closer to study them.

"Are they moonstone?" I asked her.

Her eyes were soft with sentiment when she turned to me. "That's right. And they're carved—can you see?—with tiny suns and moons. One of my witch sisters gave them to me. I was thinking we could incorporate these buttons into your dress. They're very meaningful."

I knew a little about crystals. I had been doing some of my witch studying in between knitting lessons and running a business and traveling with my soon-to-be husband.

I tried to remember what I'd read. "It's a relationship stone." Not a bad guess, considering a witch had used the stone on a wedding gown.

"That's right. Among other things, it should help you have smoothness in your communication."

I thought about some of the strong opinions both Rafe and I could hold and appreciated that smooth communication could come in handy.

"And the suns and moons are like Rafe and me. A creature of the day and of the night fitting together."

"Exactly," said Gran, looking pleased.

Sylvia put her head to one side. "But there are only five remaining buttons. The sixth one seems to have dropped off."

"Well, can't we make five work?" I asked. I really liked these buttons and loved the idea that they'd featured on Gran's dress too.

Sylvia said, "Not with the pattern we've chosen. You'll need at least nine."

Surely there had to be a way around this. And there was.

Clara said, "I know someone who can make them."

We all turned to stare at her. "You know someone who can make carved moonstone buttons?" I had to be sure we were talking about the same thing.

"Yes. He lives in Wallingford. I had him do some lovely carved shell buttons for a cloak I made, several years ago now. He specializes in crystals. Herrick's Crystal is a charming shop near the Sheep Market."

"Wallingford's not far," Sylvia said. "Why don't we all go? Make a road trip of it."

I loved that idea. I felt like I'd been cooped up in the shop or buried in wedding planning for too long. The sun was out, spring was springing around the land, and I longed to take a drive. "Didn't Agatha Christie live there?" It was one of those bits of trivia that I'd obviously read somewhere, and it had stuck with me.

"That's right. Her house was called Winterbrook. We can drive by it if you like. Agatha and her second husband, Max, were happy there."

"Did you know Agatha Christie?" I sometimes forgot how much of a celebrity Sylvia had been when she'd been alive and making movies.

Her expression was cool. "Darling, I knew everyone."

CHAPTER 2

We decided to go the next day, a Friday. We set out in the morning, leaving Violet in charge of the shop. She gave a long-suffering sigh when she found out she'd be stuck in the shop while I was out. Honestly, most of the time she acted like an overworked slave, when in truth she was well paid. Overpaid for the amount of work she actually did.

Sylvia liked to have a male chauffeur. And, since it was her car, we tended to let her have her way. So Alfred was called into service to drive the Bentley.

Alfred politely opened the doors and helped us all inside. When we were settled and he'd headed on his way, Sylvia said, "By the way, Lucy, if you'd like to borrow the Bentley for your wedding, you'd be most welcome."

"That's really nice of you. But I think Rafe has the transport under control."

She seemed to think about it for a minute. "Perhaps I should lend you my Cartier necklace, then, for your something borrowed."

I nearly opened the car door and threw myself out of the moving vehicle. I thought Sylvia had finally forgiven me for temporarily losing her most priceless possession, and I'd finally forgiven her for nearly getting me killed, and she was thinking about lending it to me? We were all staring at her, and a terrible silence filled the car. Then I caught the twinkle in the back of her eyes. I burst out laughing, and then, seeing the joke, the rest of us fell to giggling like, well, like a car full of women on the way to do some bridal shopping.

We were an odd bunch, but these crazy, undead women were among my closest friends.

Wallingford wasn't that far from Oxford, and we hit the outskirts of the town in about forty minutes.

"Oh, dear," Alfred said as the traffic grew hairy. "I think it's a market day in town."

"Market day?"

"Yes. Wallingford has been a market town since Saxon times."

I was always amazed at these little bits of history. I imagined people trading grain and sheepskins and whatever else they swapped more than a thousand years ago. The traffic might be crazy, but I was excited to be here on a market day. I could play tourist. We decided to visit the button guy first and then wander around the market.

Wallingford was also familiar for another reason. "I think it was in Wallingford that the witch lived, the one who sold the hex that got put on Violet."

Gran stared at me. "The Wicked Witch of Wallingford."

I'd barely finished laughing from Sylvia's joke about lending me her Cartier necklace. Now I was spurting with laughter again. "The Wicked Witch of Wallingford. That's a good one."

"I'm not being funny. If it's the same woman, I've known her for years. She was a powerful witch and not the whitest."

"She doesn't really call herself the Wicked Witch of Wallingford, does she?"

"Of course not. It's our nickname for her. Her name is Karmen. With a K," she said, as though that in itself were unseemly.

I'd been wanting to have a few words with the woman who'd nearly killed my cousin. Seemed like fate was putting me in this Karmen's orbit. "Perhaps we should drop in on her while we're here. I really want to meet the witch who sold that hex."

Alfred finally managed to find parking for the Bentley, and we all piled out. We must have looked like a very odd bunch. The female vampires all had large sun hats made out of sun-screened fabric, and Sylvia had added a parasol. Alfred made do with a fedora. I was bareheaded, though I always wore sunscreen.

The town was bustling, but even among the throngs of people I could admire the Tudor buildings and the quaint little shops that I was dying to dive into. Wallingford was on the River Thames, and I determined to come back one day when there was no market on and wander the path beside the river.

Herrick's Crystal was on St. Mary's, a pedestrian-only street crammed with gift shops, sweet shops, a wonderful bookstore and a couple of coffee shops. The little windows glinted with interesting treasures. Half eggs of amethyst geodes revealed the most gorgeous purple. There had to be every crystal imaginable from all over the world in there. Polished agates, spears of quartz, stones made into jewelry. I could feel their energy drawing me in.

We all crammed into the small shop, pretty much filling it up. Fortunately, we were the only customers. A tall, gaunt man with gray hair balding on top glanced up as we came in. He was stoop-shouldered, presumably from bending over all his life. He was inspecting a large aquamarine through a magnifying lens attached to a headband.

"Can I help you?" he asked. One pale blue eye looked inquiringly while the other was covered by the lens.

Gran took the box of moonstone buttons that she'd carefully snipped off her dress and showed them to him. He picked one up and inspected it. "Very fine work. I didn't do it, did I?"

"I don't think so." She explained that she wanted him to make four more. He looked at each button in turn and finally said, "I can't promise that my work will be as fine as this. It's exquisite. But I'll do my best. End of next week all right?"

We agreed that it was, and having executed our most important commission, we left the shop.

"Now shall we hit the market?" Clara asked.

"What a good idea," I agreed.

The market was colorful and noisy. Sylvia turned to me. "Lucy, wouldn't it be an excellent idea for you to start coming to these things? You could sell some of your knitting kits and maybe promote the classes. We could stock your stall with handcrafted sweaters, cushions, scarves and so on. It wouldn't be too far to come and could add extra income."

"That's a great idea," I said. "If I wasn't kind of busy right now. Getting married and all."

She grew quite fierce. "You must not allow your marriage to interfere with your business." She gave a little laugh. "I never did."

We took a moment to watch the hustle and bustle. I doubted whether this market had changed so very much since Saxon times. Sure, the people would be dressed differently, and the products would be mostly different, but at its heart, this was a place for people to trade goods. And I was definitely willing to take some goods off sellers' hands.

I bought some beautiful beeswax candles at one stand. Most of my candles tended to be for my craft, but these I pictured on the dining-room table at Rafe's house. I looked at pottery plates and hand-carved wooden bowls, and then I came to a table laid out with skincare products in beautiful dark blue glass jars and bottles. The table was decorated with crystals, no doubt from the crystal house we'd just left, and as they winked in the sunshine, I was drawn towards that table as though they had reached out little hands and pulled me there.

I wasn't the only one, either. It was quite a busy area. I glanced up to see who was running it and saw an astonishingly beautiful woman. In a village market full of everyday-looking people (if you ignored the vampires), she was like a storybook princess. She had black, curly hair that hung to her waist, big, dark eyes, flawless skin, and full lips painted red. She wore a lacy blue top over jeans and what looked like diamond and lapis earrings hung from her ears. She was wrapping up a jar of cream and saying to the older woman who was buying it, "Every night, remember. And I promise you, at the end of three months, you will see a difference."

The customer gazed up and said, "Will I have skin like yours?"

The woman laughed. "You never know."

She had a helper with her, a dowdy woman, much older, and as that woman helped the next customer, the dark-haired beauty turned to me. As our gazes connected, I felt a zing of recognition. It was odd. I'd never met this woman in my life. Her eyes narrowed slightly as though she'd felt it too.

"May I help you, little sister?"

So that was it. She was another witch. "I was just passing by. Your packaging is so beautiful."

She laughed softly, a husky sound. Even her teeth were perfect. "It's not the outside but what's inside that counts."

She reached out and picked up my hand, bringing it closer, and then from a pump bottle squeezed a little lotion onto my wrist. She rubbed it in, and I felt the delicious smoothness of the cream, breathed in a slight aroma that smelled like a garden in spring. No one scent stood out, but they mingled pleasantly.

"What is in this stuff?" I asked, amazed.

"My secret recipe."

There were night creams, day creams, cleansers, and lip balms. She had sample packs containing a small bottle of each and a small zip-up bag to contain them all. As she saw me looking at them, the witch said, "Those make excellent bridesmaid gifts."

Even though we were both witches, I couldn't believe she could read my mind so perfectly. "How did you know that's what I was thinking?"

She chuckled. "Your engagement ring sparkles with newness, and there's no wedding band. Educated guess."

"Well, you're correct. I'm a bride-to-be." Maybe that sounded corny, but I didn't care. I even liked using the word fiancé. No doubt some day in the future I'd refer to Rafe as my hubby. The thought of his face if I said it made me want to practice straightaway.

The other witch said, "If you give me the names of your attendants, I'll have the bags personalized. We make them to order. I can have them ready for you by next week. Is that soon enough?"

"That's fantastic. Thank you." I gave her Alice, Violet, and Jennifer's names. Then added Olivia as a thanks to Olivia Thresher, as she was doing the flowers.

And, since I was as vain as the next woman, I decided to buy some cream for myself as well.

"You don't live near here," she said with certainty.

I shook my head. "I'm from Oxford."

Her gaze sharpened on mine. "You know Margaret Twigg, then."

And if there was ever a connection that wasn't going to make me warm to this woman, it was knowing Margaret Twigg. Still, the leader of my coven was certainly well-known in witching circles, so I couldn't hold that against this woman.

"I do."

She laughed again, that husky laugh. "I can tell from your tone that Margaret isn't your favorite among our sisters."

Now I felt mean. "It's not that, it's just—"

She patted my wrist. "No need to explain. And what is your name?"

"I'm Lucy Swift."

"Ah. I have heard of you."

"You have?" That did not sound like good news.

Her lips twitched. "You own a knitting shop, I believe. I've been meaning to get down there. I like to knit in the evenings while I'm watching TV."

That sounded like such a domestic occupation for this glamorous woman. "You'd be welcome anytime," I said.

"I'm Karmen."

Her eyes widened and went to where her fingers were still resting on my wrist. My pulse must have jumped when I heard her name. "Do you know ill of me?"

Only that my grandmother had referred to her as the Wicked Witch of Wallingford, and I strongly suspected her of selling the hex that nearly killed Violet. I wasn't going to have it out with her here in public. I drew my hand back and said, "May I come and visit you later? I'd love to see your operation."

Her eyes narrowed ever so slightly, and then she relaxed into a smile. "You'd be most welcome, little sister. Shall we say four o'clock? You can choose the fabric for your bags. Tilda, my assistant, makes them."

Hearing her name, the assistant looked over inquiringly. She was probably in her sixties and had a slightly anxious expression on her wrinkled face. Tendrils of gray hair escaped from the bun at her nape, and she brushed a curl off her cheek. "Bridesmaid gifts," Karmen said.

Tilda smiled at me. "Congratulations on your wedding. Yes, I'll custom make the bags for you. Those sets make lovely gifts for the bridal attendants."

Karmen said, "My address is on my card."

I nodded. "See you at four."

I wished I hadn't gotten so carried away now. Would Violet really want cream made by this woman whose hex had made her hair and teeth fall out? Would it be lying if I simply didn't mention where I'd purchased the cream from? I was going to use mine immediately, so I'd be product-testing before it went near my bridesmaids.

CHAPTER 3

I turned away from the witch's stall and noticed Gran was no longer standing at my elbow. I glanced around and saw her a few stalls away, pretending to look at crocheted bedspreads. Even from here, I could see they were nothing like as good as what Gran could make herself in a single night. When she saw me looking her way, she motioned me over. I caught up with her, and she tugged my arm and pulled me into the crowd.

"What's going on? You're acting so weird."

"I know that witch."

"Really?" That was unfortunate. It would really put a damper on her day because we'd thought we'd be safe bringing Gran out to Wallingford. She got restless stuck inside all the time and only being able to walk outside at night. Of course, we weren't far from Oxford, so it wasn't that surprising she'd see someone she'd known in life. We really needed to think about getting Gran a lot farther away if she was going to manage a more normal existence.

Gran looked more perplexed than I would have expected catching a glimpse of someone she used to know. It shouldn't be that big a deal. And it didn't seem like the other witch had seen her. Then she said, "Lucy, Karmen is older than I am."

I let out a snort of disbelief. "No offense, but that woman must be her daughter."

She shook her head. "Karmen never had children. It's her. I'm certain of it."

I surreptitiously looked back at the skincare booth. Karmen didn't only have young-looking skin and hair, but even her posture, the fluidity of her movements, were not those of an old person. "Gran, that woman can't be more than forty."

"Her face belies her age."

"Do you think she's had a lot of work done?"

Gran looked at me questioningly. "Work?"

"You know. Facelifts and other cosmetic surgeries."

She shook her head. "It's more than that. Be very careful with that one."

"Could she be like you? Undead?" But Karmen had greeted me witch to witch and had none of the characteristics I'd come to associate with vampires. In fact, she'd rubbed cream into my wrist, and her fingers had been warm.

"No. She's still mortal, of that I'm sure."

"Are there spells that can keep you young?" And if there were, I really wanted to hear about them.

She flicked a glance at me and looked worried. "Not really, my dear. But there are other arts. Not of witchery so much as alchemy."

"Alchemy? Isn't that turning lead into gold?"

"Turning that which is base into that which is pure. Worthless metal into gold, but more importantly, mortal flesh into immortal."

"Mortal flesh into immortal?"

She nodded.

I felt a shiver go down the back of my neck. And not in a pleasant way. "Are you trying to tell me that woman may have found the elusive fountain of youth?"

"Not found it. Created it."

Suddenly those pots and potions seemed a whole lot more interesting to me. "And she's selling it in bottles?"

Gran shook her head. "She's not sharing what she knows. It would be too dangerous."

Still, I was intrigued. As a mortal woman about to marry a vampire, a potion that could keep me young would be pretty interesting.

Sylvia came up then and grabbed at our elbows. "What are you two doing waltzing off without me?"

Quickly and in a low voice, Gran explained everything she'd just told me.

Sylvia glanced at me and then back the way we'd come, to where the witch's booth was doing a roaring trade. "What a perfect solution for you, Lucy."

Gran's face was creased in worry. "I'm not so sure. I'm not at all sure it's a good idea to meddle in alchemy. We witches work with the natural energy in the world. We don't try to pervert nature's course."

But I wanted to know more. "So does she just look young and still live her regular span of years? Or will the elixir of youth keep her young forever?"

"I never studied it very deeply," Gran said, "but I believe it will keep her young as long as she keeps taking the elixir. She can still be killed by accident or disease, you understand, but not old age."

Alchemy was one of the many things I knew very little about. "I thought the alchemist created a stone or something. Isn't it also called the philosopher's stone?"

"That's right. The philosopher's stone is a substance made of a number of ingredients that the alchemist keeps very secret. If it even exists. It can be a stone. It can also be a powder. The true secret of alchemy isn't turning base matter into precious metal; it's eternal youth. But a little of the elixir of life must be taken on a regular basis or it will wear off."

I didn't want to get into a big discussion about alchemy with Gran in the middle of a crowded marketplace, but I was interested. I had to admit, I was interested. This could be the solution to the biggest conflict that Rafe and I were going to have in our relationship. I didn't want to turn into a vampire, but what if I could stay young-looking and extend my natural lifespan? That could be cool. Though I could see that it would be fraught with certain difficulties too. However, it was worth thinking about.

Sylvia was much more positive about the whole elixir of youth thing than my grandmother seemed to be. She said brightly, "Well, you must ask her about it."

Gran looked grimly at both of us. "Don't forget that the reason you wanted to speak to her is that you suspect Karmen sold the hex that nearly killed your cousin."

I admit momentarily I had been so dazzled by the idea of eternal youth that I'd completely forgotten the hex thing. "It doesn't put her in the best light, does it?"

Once again, Sylvia turned the conversation in a more positive direction. "I still think it would be a good idea to find out what she knows about this youth-inducing potion. If you don't ask her, I certainly will."

Gran looked like she would argue and then merely said, "I can't go with you, much as I'd like to. She didn't see me, but if she did, I'm sure she would recognize me."

"And you don't want her to know you're a vampire."

"The less she knows about any of us, the better."

It was unlike Gran to be so mysterious and dark. She said, "I wish you wouldn't go. I have a bad feeling in my waters."

She must really have a bad feeling if she was bringing up her waters. It was a weird, old-fashioned expression that she only used when she was seriously perturbed.

Sylvia said, "Well, you rest your waters in the Bentley. Take Alfred with you. He'd only be in the way. Lucy and I will go and see this witch."

"What about Clara and Mabel?"

She shook her head and said tartly, "Those bunglers. Best they stay out of it."

So we decided that Alfred and the other three vampires would visit the Sheep Market, an old coaching inn that was now an indoor collection of antique stalls, while Sylvia and I went to see the witch.

I'd expected to be called into chauffeur duty, since Alfred was busy chaperoning the female vampires, but Sylvia drove the Bentley. I'd never seen her drive before. It suited her, and I told her so.

She glanced at me, not looking best pleased. "It suits me to sit in the back and be chauffeured, like the film star I am."

"Right. What was I thinking?" The world might have

29

moved on, but Sylvia never forgot that she'd been a glamorous celebrity back in her heyday.

We drove a little way out of town and then down a lane, and at the end of it was a long, low thatched cottage with several outbuildings. It was oddly shaped for a house, and it wasn't a farm. As she turned off the engine, Sylvia said, "Why, it's an old pub." And then I saw that she was right. But there was a cottage next door where presumably the publican had once lived. There was smoke coming from the chimney.

We got out of the car and headed for the cottage. No sign of a doorbell, so I lifted a brass door knocker shaped like a lion's head and banged it against the old black front door. I could hear the knock echoing inside the house.

There was no answer, so I tried again. And then Karmen popped her head out of the door of the old pub and said, "We're in here."

I was disappointed because I wanted to see inside the cute cottage, but Sylvia and I walked to the pub and through the door Karmen was holding open. It was a large space with plenty of windows, though they were small, mullioned windows. The floor was wood, stained and scarred by age and spilled beer—oak, I thought. The long bar remained but was obviously more of a workspace. In front was a workshop and retail store. Where once there would have been bottles of alcohol, now there were pots and jars of skin products. Karmen and her assistant were unloading the leftovers from the market. I smelled the same light scent I'd noticed when Karmen rubbed her hand cream onto my wrist. I introduced Sylvia to Karmen and watched them take stock of each other. Two powerful, vain creatures. Would they bond or loathe each other on sight? It was impossible to tell, as they were both coolly polite.

"What a gorgeous space," I said, looking around.

"Thank you. Come and see the kitchen. It's where I brew my potions."

The old pub kitchen mixed the old with the new. I could swear I still smelled old hops, but I also smelled herbs, noting the top notes of licorice and rosemary. A big gas stove and a series of pots suggested she really produced her creams right here. Hanging from a clothes line were bundles of drying herbs, while jars and bottles and sacks and bags of curious-looking ingredients were stacked neatly on the open shelves. The décor was curious. The walls had been painted terracotta and stenciled in black and gold. There was a slogan in what I assumed was Latin, with a curious symbol beside it. Like two triangles intersecting. Rafe could translate the saying, but I didn't want to snap a photo while Karmen was standing beside me.

We remained pleasant while she showed us around and then she said, "Tilda, take Lucy to choose the fabric for her bags."

"Of course," Tilda said, immediately abandoning her unpacking duties to do what her boss told her. I wished Violet could witness such excellent employee behavior.

Tilda took me out to the main pub area, where a long wooden pub table sat empty. I pictured women packaging the pots so vividly, I suspected that's what the table was used for. She kept going, and in a corner alcove under a window was a fancy sewing machine and a modern cabinet beside it. She opened a drawer and revealed a selection of fabrics. Her hands moved over them. "Mother's Day, gifts for teachers, ah, here we are. Brides." And she lifted a stack of samples.

Sylvia was instantly bored and drifted away. The fabrics were all pretty and ranged from prints with cocktail glasses and lipsticks to hearts and doves and, finally, a selection of floral patterns. I chose a print with pink roses on a green background.

"What do you think?" I asked Tilda, holding up the sample.

"I think it would be beautiful. I'll enjoy working on the bags for your wedding. What a joyful thing a wedding is." She held her ringless left hand up. "Not that I was ever so fortunate. I was never a beauty. 'If you can't be pretty, be useful,' my mother always said. And so I learned to cook and sew and mend things. With no man about to help me, I've learned to do most things for myself."

She didn't sound sorry for herself, just matter-of-fact. I had no idea how to respond and luckily didn't have to. Karmen returned.

"Come back to my cottage, and I'll make you some tea."

I was pleased to get into that lovely-looking thatched cottage, and also, I wanted to talk to her about that hex, and I preferred to do it without a mortal assistant listening in.

As she led us in through that black door, I felt something in the air. Like a quiver of dark energy. And yet the décor was beautiful. It was like a high-end B&B with overstuffed chintz chairs and gleaming antique furniture. Tasteful paintings graced the walls, and a basket of wool with a partially completed sweater sat beside a comfortable couch. A fire was laid in the big fireplace under a black-beamed mantel. With a snap of her fingers, she set the blaze going. The walls were painted a rich, buttery cream, and the flagstone floors were covered with plush carpets. The ancient beams crisscrossed above our heads, and the fireplace was done in an old herringbone brick pattern. I was no expert, but I was fairly certain this was mostly original Tudor.

As I gazed around, I said, "Your home is beautiful."

And yet there was that strange sensation of chill darkness that wafted over me now and then. It was as though I were standing in a field of lavender and then caught a whiff of skunk. Strange feeling.

She busied herself in the kitchen and then returned carrying a tray containing blue and gold china mugs, not teacups, I was pleased to note. I still hadn't gotten used to the tiny amount of liquid available from a teacup.

I sniffed the brew appreciatively. It's kind of a witch thing. We all had our own special recipes, and hers contained lavender, rosehips, that hint of licorice, and other things that I couldn't distinguish. I took a sip and definitely approved. It was a rich blend with a hint of spice.

"This is delicious," I said.

Sylvia either took a cautious sip or pretended to and then agreed that it was very nice. I knew that I was either going to end up drinking her tea as well as mine or she'd chuck it in a nearby potted plant when Karmen was out of the room.

We three settled in chintz armchairs, and then Karmen said, "Tell me about yourself."

But this wasn't really a social visit. I paused and said, "I'm part of a coven in Oxford led by Margaret Twigg."

Her glorious full lips thinned slightly. "Ah, yes. Margaret. She does keep coming up."

"She's the head of my coven and sort of a mentor." When

she wasn't being a pain in my behind. "We recently had to reverse a hex that we think you may have sold."

Her lips tilted in a pleasant smile, and I could see the amusement lurking at the back of her big, almond eyes. Had I really expected her to apologize?

"I sell a great many hexes." And didn't sound the tiniest bit guilty that she did so.

"This one almost killed my assistant, who is also my cousin. Perhaps you recognize it? It was a goat's skull with various symbols scribbled on it and the words '*Grow ugly, wither and die*' written in reverse. Does this ring any bells?"

If anything, her amusement deepened. "You sound so fierce, I'm nearly frightened. As I said, I sell many hexes. And I'm fairly certain your cousin isn't dead. I'd have heard."

And I was fairly certain I wasn't getting through to her. I couldn't believe this woman. I leaned forward. "No thanks to you."

She made a tsking sound. "Come now, Lucy. You're not that naïve. You know as well as I do that often spells and curses are metaphorical."

"There was nothing metaphorical about what happened to Vi. I saw her hair falling out. Her teeth were falling out. She was getting these horrible skin breakouts. And then we reversed the curse and sent it back where it came from, and the—" Here I looked at her directly. "And the person who bought that hex from you did die."

Honestly, you'd think I was doing a stand-up routine, the way she seemed to find me so amusing. "But she didn't die from the hex. I do keep up with the news, Lucy. That woman was murdered."

34

"So you did sell her the hex." Ha, she'd as good as admitted it. Was I good at subtle interrogation or what?

She shrugged her shoulders. "The murdered woman's photograph was in the paper and on television. She looked familiar."

I felt like I really wasn't getting anywhere. "What about our first rule, do no harm?"

Her beautifully penciled eyebrows rose. "And what about the equally potent advice to be careful what you wish for?"

"But if I hadn't reversed the hex—"

She interrupted me. "Yes. If you hadn't interfered, it would have been much better. How dare you get involved in things you don't understand? To manipulate spells that were not of your own creation."

Wait a minute. How had we gone from me accusing her of being a bad witch to her turning it back on me? I felt like yet another curse had been reversed. And this time I was the victim.

"I think what Lucy means," Sylvia interrupted silkily, "is that we admire your work greatly. However, if a hex is intended for another witch in Oxford, it would be courteous to let the local witches know of it."

That wasn't at all what I'd meant, but it did smooth over an awkward moment. And I supposed Sylvia had a point. I couldn't stop the woman from selling hexes, but at least if she was selling them in my neighborhood, I'd like to know about it. So I nodded.

Karmen sat back. "All right. That seems fair. And—" She raised a finger. Even her hands were perfect. The skin soft and the oval fingernails painted soft pink. How did she do that? Between making potions and practicing with my dagger and running a knitting shop, my hands were always dry and a little rough. "You agree to do the same. If you plan to sell any of your wares here, you'll let me know."

The only thing I might sell in Wallingford was wool and knitting kits, but I didn't think she'd care about those, so I said nothing and sipped more tea.

Karmen had been sending frequent glances Sylvia's way and finally asked, "What is your skin-care regime? Your complexion is remarkable for a woman your age. If I may say so."

Sylvia never liked to be reminded that she hadn't been a young woman when she'd been turned. Still, she was beautiful in a silver-haired, Helen Mirren way.

Her smile was brittle as she answered, "My secret is that I think only positive thoughts."

I had to bite my tongue to stop myself from bursting out with laughter. That was not the Sylvia I knew.

"And of course," Sylvia added sweetly, "I stay out of the sun."

Good thing I wasn't drinking tea at the time or I'd have snorted it up my nose. The witch nodded. "Absolutely. Nothing ages us like sun damage." Then she turned her attention to me. "I hope you're using sunscreen every day. You're what, thirty?"

"Not quite." I had my feminine vanity too. Okay, my next birthday would be my thirtieth, but I was hanging on to my twenties as hard as I could. I was happy that my wedding would come first.

In my turn, I gushed. "And your skin looks amazing, too," I said to the witch. "And you're, what, forty? What's your secret?" Oh, two could play the how-old-are-you game.

The glance she shot me was both calculating and amused. "I always think age is a state of mind, don't you? And my skin products will definitely help keep you young."

"Lucy's getting married soon," Sylvia said. "Do you have anything special to help her stay young-looking?"

I nearly choked on my tea. What was she doing?

However, Karmen looked delighted. Or pretended to look delighted. Hard to tell yet which it was. She jumped to her feet. "Absolutely. I'm going to give you a jar of my best face cream. It's got SPF50. It will keep your skin looking dewy and help prevent that sun damage we were talking about."

She got up and left the room, and with the ease of frequent practice, Sylvia and I swapped mugs. There was about a quarter cup of tea left in mine, which now sat in front of the vampire. I gulped down as much of Sylvia's tea as I could before the witch returned, holding one of her blue glass jars, although the label on this one was different. It had extra writing on it in gold.

"This is from my private collection," she said with a significant look. "I put a little extra in this."

I chuckled. "I'm not above a little magic if it will keep me looking younger." But was it really going to last for forty years? I was suspicious.

I opened the lid of her private collection cream and sniffed. It smelled wonderful.

I had to wonder how she ran her business with so few staff. When I asked her, she looked at me seriously.

"We must be very careful. I could expand my line of skincare and have it mass-produced and sold all over the world, but I choose very deliberately to keep the business small. There's only me and my assistant, Tilda."

"Wow. You do everything, just the two of you?"

"Yes. When it's very busy, we hire extra help, but only to box and ship things. I keep my secrets guarded closely, and so should you."

I felt that shiver again. What secrets did I have in my business? Okay, the vampire knitting club was extremely hush-hush, but the shop itself was nothing special. However, she'd hinted that her cream had magical properties, and I didn't think that was just advertising hype.

"Is your assistant a witch too?" I was pretty sure she wasn't, but I couldn't always tell.

She shook her head. "No. Tilda can follow my recipes exactly though." Her eyes glittered as she looked at me. Then she turned her head as though to make sure her assistant hadn't sneaked in while we were talking. Even though it was just the three of us, she lowered her voice. "But when she's done, I add a couple of extra secret ingredients she knows nothing about. That way she can never steal my recipes. You see? One must always be vigilant. In work and in life."

I thought it was a cynical attitude, but I kept my mouth shut. This woman had been a practicing witch longer than I had. A lot longer if Gran was right. I should probably pay attention.

Then I tried to imagine Violet stealing my secrets and nearly laughed. Vi was more interested in working as few hours as possible for the maximum paycheck possible. My business secrets were mine to keep.

But then Gran had been a witch for a really long time, too. She'd never seemed to have that attitude. Gran was open and giving. From her cookie recipes to her knitting patterns, she was always willing to share.

And if anyone had come to her looking for a hex, she would have sent them on their way with a sharp word of warning.

I'd much rather model myself on my grandmother than this frighteningly young-looking witch.

CHAPTER 4

When we returned to Oxford, it was after six. Nyx acted like I'd been gone for a year instead of an afternoon, so I spent some time fussing over her and feeding her before heading down to the shop. Violet had closed Cardinal Woolsey's, but I wanted to make sure everything was tidy, and to see if she'd left me any notes about anything that needed doing.

I flipped on the lights, and there was a note from Violet. She'd sold a lot of the sock yarn I'd talked about in my last newsletter. I was going to have to remember to order extra of the products I highlighted in the newsletter. It was an obvious thing to do, but I was still finding my way and cautious about overordering stock. I set to work preparing an order, and as I was working, someone rapped on the front door. This was annoying. The closed sign was clearly visible, but sometimes people thought if they saw lights on, I might let them in anyway. Depending on who was at the front door, I sometimes did.

I went towards the door and peeked out to see two familiar looking people standing there.

I opened the door wide. They weren't customers.

They were my parents.

As she came inside, my mother clapped her hands and laughed, looking delighted. "Surprise!" She turned to my dad. "Oh, look at her face. We definitely got her this time."

I tried to change my expression from one of shock to delight. "What are you doing here?"

"We came early to help plan your wedding," Mom cried. "You're my only daughter, and I couldn't bear to think of you planning your wedding without me."

"But I'm not getting married for weeks yet." Behind her, my dad looked like he'd been dragged away from things he'd rather be doing.

"Exactly. Oh, what fun we'll have." Dad came in, and I looked behind them for luggage.

Mom said, "Oh, don't worry. We're not staying with you. Your father has a colleague who is working in New York for a few weeks. He's lent us his flat. Isn't that jolly?"

"Just jolly," I said. It wasn't that I didn't love my parents. I did. But my mother was a woman of strong opinions and a witch in denial, which could be challenging. Besides, my wedding was going to be small. William could plan an event better than I could and definitely better than my mother, who was a woman of intellect, not practicality. I glanced at my dad, and he lifted and dropped his shoulders imperceptibly. This had definitely not been his idea.

Before I could ask them anything more, Mom said, "And we have another surprise for you."

"I'm not sure I can take any more surprises."

Then, as though they'd been hovering around the corner waiting, two more people came through the door and into the shop. "Meri! And Pete!" I hugged them both.

Meri was short for Meritamun. She'd been an Egyptian witch trapped in a magical mirror for a very long time when I helped her escape. She'd been my shop assistant for a while, a very willing worker, but it was difficult to get somebody comfortable with an electronic cash register when they came from the time of the abacus.

Pete was an Australian Egyptologist who'd managed to get work with my parents on their dig in Egypt. Meri had gone back with them, and her knowledge of the Middle Kingdom was invaluable.

Mother looked around. "I see your little shop hasn't changed. But then it never does. I think it looks the same as it did when my mother ran it."

I was never certain whether she intended to insult me when she said things like this. My mom had made no secret that she felt I should be doing more important work than running a little knitting shop in Oxford. I disagreed. I was proud of Cardinal Woolsey's and what I'd achieved with it. But I was never going to change her mind. I thought by now she realized she wasn't going to change mine, either. I wouldn't suddenly chuck in the knitting shop and go into law, or politics, or medicine, or, horror of horrors, archaeology to be just like them.

They'd met Rafe when they'd last been in Oxford and had renewed their acquaintance with him when we'd visited them in Egypt to tell them we were engaged. At least in my marriage, they couldn't fault me. Rafe was pretty much an ambitious mother's dream groom for her daughter. He was rich, handsome, and probably best of all to my parents, he taught occasionally at university. He was a world-renowned expert on old manuscripts. He and my dad could spend a whole evening discussing the Dead Sea Scrolls, and even though my eyeballs would be falling out of my head from boredom, they'd both love every minute of it.

Mom looked around as though wondering where everybody was. "And where's this soon to be son-in-law of mine? I can't wait to give him a big hug and a kiss."

"He had meetings this afternoon. I'm not sure where he is right now."

"We thought we'd go to the pub up the street for dinner. You will come along with us?"

"Of course." I was definitely hungry. And now that I'd recovered from my initial shock, it was nice to see my parents.

It was an easy walk from the shop up to the pub, so we left by the front door, and I locked up. Meri hung back to walk with me. In her soft voice, she said, "I am very happy for you. If you would like me to stay as your handmaid, I would be honored."

This was the thing about Meri. Even though she'd been in the modern world for over a year now, she quickly defaulted to her former position as a servant. Still, I was genuinely touched.

"I appreciate that so much. But my mom and dad need you on the dig. You know more about the history than anyone alive."

"Because it is not history to me. I lived in that time."

"I know. But you don't really want to come back to England, do you?"

"For you, Lucy, I would brave anything. I owe you my life."

I shook my head. I'd tried and tried to get through to her about this point. "You don't owe me anything. We're sister witches. It's a shared bond."

"Know this," she said, her eyes huge and dark and so serious. "I'm yours to command at any time."

"And I appreciate that so much." And so hoped I never would have to take her up on it. Meri had been through enough.

"He's a good man, the one you marry," she said. "Even if he is a creature of the dark."

"And we don't ever say that to Mom and Dad, right?"

I'd finally done something right in my mother's eyes, marrying the perfect guy. I didn't want to spoil it all by her discovering he was a vampire.

Meri laughed. "As you moderns would say, my lips are sealed."

She looked much better than the last time I'd seen her. She was getting used to life in this crazy world. Also, she seemed to be very comfortable in Pete's company. "Speaking of romance, how's it going with Pete?"

She giggled and blushed. "I like him very much. Even though he does not take his craft as seriously as I do, he makes me laugh."

Pete had that jokey, Aussie bloke way about him, but I'd seen him take his craft very seriously. He was one of the reasons that Meri was alive today.

Dinner was actually a lot of fun. Pete was funny and entertaining as always. And Mom and Dad were still riding on the high of having so successfully surprised me. They caught me up on the news of their dig, and then Mom said, "But enough about us. Tell me all your plans for the wedding.

And tell me I'm in time for your hen party? In fact, I'm hoping to help organize it. I've got plenty of ideas."

She looked so thrilled at the idea of a hen party that I didn't want to tell her I'd begged Violet not to have one. I'd been disturbed too many nights by boisterous groups of hens partying around Oxford at night. However, I didn't feel like having an argument with my mother right this minute. She and Violet could sort it out later.

And then, as if that wasn't bad enough, my dad said, "And Pete, we must see about Rafe's bachelor party."

"Dad, I really don't think he's having one."

My father looked shocked. "Then it's a good thing we came here." He turned to my mom. "You were right after all, my dear. Why, a man must have a bachelor party. It's a rite of passage."

"Too right," Pete said.

Suddenly, eloping became very appealing.

∾

I QUIETLY SENT an emergency text to Rafe. I was powerless against these people who had either birthed me, offered to be my handmaiden or, in the case of Pete, helped save my mother's life. I needed someone who could shut down his bachelor party without offending anyone. Or, at least, if he offended them, then I didn't have to.

My text read, *"Mayday. Mayday. Parents arrived unexpectedly. Dad wants to throw you a bachelor party. Rescue me. We're at the Bishop's Mitre."*

Then, having decided there wasn't much else I could do to avert wedding disasters, I perused the menu. Okay, I knew the menu backwards and forwards, but at least reading it one more time gave me a second to find my balance. Taking my cue, everyone else paused and started reading the menu too.

"Lucy, what's good here?" my mother asked.

"Mom. You've eaten here. The menu hasn't changed very much."

My father jumped in before we could start bickering. "I for one long for some good British cooking. The food on the archaeological dig frankly often tastes like something we've dug up."

Well, there was an image to put me off my food. Not really. I told everyone in a loud, bright voice that I would have the fish and chips. I've often found that the minute one person gets decisive, everybody else jumps on board. Sure enough, my dad nodded, removed his spectacles and said, "And I'm for the sausage and mash." He gazed around fondly at the rest of us as though we were new students in one of his study groups. "No matter how far one travels, one always longs for one's native cuisine."

Dad had been a student here in Oxford. It was how he and my mother met—he the young American grad student, she the British student who shared his enthusiasm for archaeology.

Pete shut his menu next. "There's a hamburger that'll do me nicely."

Mother said she was torn between shepherd's pie and soup and salad. Meri stared at the menu, looking confused. She'd had very little experience with restaurants, not helped by the fact that she'd lived many months on an archaeological dig in Egypt where they struggled to get internet and gourmet food was a pretty low priority. I doubted she visited many restaurants.

I leaned closer to her. I tried to remember if she was vegetarian and couldn't. But I recalled that she preferred simple foods. I pointed her to the vegetarian risotto. "I hear that's very nice."

She nodded at me, looking grateful. "Then that is what I shall have."

Dad got up, ready to go to the bar and order our food. "Come on, Mother," he said. "You're holding us all up. And I for one am hungry."

"Oh, hold your horses. I'll have the salad and the shepherd's pie." She looked very pleased with herself that she'd made a decision. And then she smiled up at my dad as though letting him in on a great secret. "I'll have the soup for lunch another day."

"Excellent decision," said the man who'd lived with her for decades.

Now that I was getting more accustomed to the idea of my parents and Meri and Pete being here, I loosened up a little. I tried to ask more questions about the dig, which I'd much rather talk about than hen parties. Mom seemed like now that she was out of Egypt, she didn't want to talk about her favorite subject. Instead, she got a very laser-like, beady-eyed stare.

"Your wedding dress. What have you done about your wedding dress?"

I opened my mouth to tell her that the vampires were crocheting me one and then closed my mouth so fast, my teeth snapped together. What was I thinking? And one more panicked text went out to Gran and Sylvia, assuming that one of them would have their phones with them, warning that Mom was in town and Gran was going to have to stay out of sight.

Gran played a large role in my life since the shop had been hers before me, and we talked every day. I was going to have to get rid of Gran's gingersnap cookies, too, before my mom came up to the flat. I'd fooled her once, telling her that I'd found Gran's recipe. But, if pressed, I'd have a hard time making a batch of cookies that tasted like my grandmother's. Besides, I didn't have time to bake. I had a wedding to plan, a business to run, and now, as though I didn't have enough to do, I had to entertain my parents and keep them out of the vampire zone.

Life had suddenly become a lot more complicated. And it wasn't an uncomplicated life to begin with.

"What an age it is since we've seen you," my mother said. This was completely untrue, as Rafe and I had visited them right after he took me to Paris, as promised.

My dad reminded her of that fact, and she waved him off. "No, not that. I mean what an age it seems since we were here seeing you."

Pete and I shared a horrified glance. The last time we'd all been together, a dreadful demon had nearly killed the lot of us. Partly, it was my mother's own fault. She had witch blood just like I did, but she'd been in denial her whole life. And that untapped power had been easy for someone with evil intent to take hold of and use against us. Did she really not remember? Or had she shoved that bad experience down in whatever vault she kept all her magic?

Not a question I wanted to pose just at the moment, obviously.

It wasn't too long before a server arrived, bearing a large tray with our food.

Few things cheered me up as quickly as English fish and chips when it was well done with nice, crispy batter and thick chips, which I still thought of as french fries but managed to refer to as chips. I was getting so English, you'd hardly know I wasn't the real deal.

"See you haven't lost any of your American accent," Pete said, immediately bursting my bubble.

I looked up at him, laughing. "You should talk. You certainly haven't picked up any Egyptian."

"Too right." He looked very proudly at Meri. "But look at Meri there. Her modern English is getting so good, you can hardly tell she doesn't have a similar background to the other grad students."

Meri looked down and shook her head bashfully. "I do make a dreadful lot of mistakes."

Since my parents were talking together, I could say softly, "Meri, you've got two thousand years of progress to catch up on. I think you're doing remarkably well."

She looked up then and beamed at me. We made our way happily through our meal, catching up and getting more comfortable with each other by the minute. Mother complimented me on the shepherd's pie as though I'd made it myself, but I liked to see her in such a good mood. It would make it easier when I had to tell her there was not going to be a bachelorette party. Or a hen party. Or anything where I had to wear embarrassing clothing and get drunk and make a spectacle of myself.

We'd reached the coffee stage when, to my great relief, I saw a tall, handsome figure striding our way. My heart still did a foolish leap every time I saw him. I wondered if that would ever end and hoped it wouldn't.

I had the pleasure of noticing the minute Rafe caught sight of me. His whole face lightened, and he picked up the pace a little. Soon he was by my side, planting a swift kiss on my lips, and then as his face brushed past my ear he whispered, "Don't worry." And somehow, now that he was here, I felt that if my worry wasn't gone, it was at least halved.

"Lovely to see you all again," he said and shook each hand around the table. He dragged a chair over from an empty table, and I shifted over, making room for him.

Dad said, "I'm glad to see you, son." Then he chuckled in a self-conscious way. "It's an odd word for me to say. But I look forward to getting used to it."

"And so do I," Rafe said. I was pleased to see he didn't add "Dad" or "Father" at the end of it. My dad had no way of knowing that Rafe was his senior by almost five hundred years.

My mother leaned forward eagerly. "You'll join us for dinner?"

He shook his head. "Thank you, but I've already eaten."

My dad got up. "Have a drink then. Or coffee at least."

"Thank you. I'll have a glass of red wine, if I may."

Dad happily went off to procure it for him, and he withstood Pete's teasing and my mom's impertinent questions with good grace. Better, in fact, than I had.

My dad returned with his glass of wine and then said, "I'm glad to see you tonight, Rafe. We must talk about your bachelor party. Now I've got some ideas—"

"That's very kind of you, but my best man will be organizing an event. The details of which, of course, he hasn't shared with me." He sent a half-amused, half-horrified glance around as though he might be subjected to strippers and lap dances. I was fairly certain that wasn't going to happen.

"Your best man. Excellent." If Dad was disappointed, he didn't show it. "Anyone I know?"

"Lochlan Balfour. He's coming down from Ireland."

As one, everyone turned to stare at him. "Lochlan Balfour?" my dad repeated. Dad was rarely starstruck by anybody who hadn't dug up something smelly and skeletal that had historical significance, so to see him getting excited by Rafe's best friend was surprising.

My mom piped up. "You don't mean Lochlan Balfour, the technology mogul?"

"The very one."

"But I thought he lived in New York," my mom said.

My dad shook his head. "Seattle."

Pete argued that they both had it wrong and his head-quarters were in Sydney.

Meri was the only one who didn't hazard an opinion. Though she clearly knew of him when she said, "He is a very famous man. I have read about him on my computer."

Rafe nodded. "He travels to all the places you mentioned for his business. Best if you don't go spreading around the news that he lives a good part of his year in Ireland. He tries to stay out of the spotlight." Or the daylight. Lochlan was another vampire, and he was older than Rafe.

"Good Lord. Imagine you knowing a fancy chap like that," Dad said.

I blinked. As fancy chaps went, Rafe wasn't half bad either.

"Well, yes, if Lochlan Balfour's organizing your bachelor

do, there's no more to be said," my dad said, sounding disappointed.

Rafe also must have heard the disappointment, for he said, "I'm sure he'd value your input and probably your help since you're in Oxford. I'll put you in touch with him."

That perked my dad up immeasurably. Whether it was because he could help plan the stag or just because he wanted to talk to a tech billionaire who was a household name, I didn't know.

My mom looked at me then. "And I suppose I'll have to speak to Violet, will I? To help plan your hen party?"

"Sure," I said weakly. I'd have to impress upon Violet how very much I did not want a hen party and leave it to her to talk my mom out of it. With any luck, some new mummified pharaoh would be discovered and that would take Mom's attention away from me, at least until the wedding.

"And who are your other attendants, dear? I don't think you said."

"Well, there's Violet, obviously; Alice, who's married to Charlie, and they have the bookshop across the street; and Jennifer's coming."

At the mention of Jennifer, who was the only person coming from the States, Mom's mouth turned down. "I do wish you'd let us invite more of our friends and family from Boston. It seems so very peculiar." Not the first time she'd aired this complaint.

With as much patience as I could muster, I said, "Mom. My life is here now. I've hardly kept in touch with anyone from back home, and you and Dad have been in Egypt a lot more than you've been in America for the last five years. Having Uncle Joe and Aunt Bessie at my wedding isn't going to mean anything to me, and two big, fat plane fares for them. And you know how cheap they are. If they actually came, they'd do nothing but complain about how much it cost until Dad wrote them a check to reimburse them."

My father looked horrified at that notion. "I think Lucy's right, Susan. Nothing wrong with a small wedding. Nothing at all."

"But she's our only daughter. She'll only get married once." And then she glanced between the two of us and in a soft voice said, "I hope."

Rafe and I both have very good hearing, but even as we chose to ignore her soft-voiced dig, his hand reached over for mine and gave it a squeeze. There would only be one marriage, and we both knew it. At least for me, but I shut that idea out of my head as quickly as it arrived.

Luckily, my parents were tired from their travels, and so dinner broke up fairly early. Pete and Meri were staying with some of Pete's Oxford friends, so amazingly my guest room was still free. It wasn't that I would have minded having a guest, but the vampire knitting club—wedding dress edition —were meeting at ten, and it might have been awkward.

After Rafe gave my dad Lochlan Balfour's contact information, we bade the four of them goodbye, and then Rafe and I turned back towards my shop. As we neared the door, he said, "Your grandmother and Sylvia both texted me to see what my plans were tonight." He looked down at me with a puzzled expression. "Is there some reason they don't want me here?"

I bit my lip. I didn't want to tell him they were making my wedding dress. I thought that was part of the surprise for the big day. "There's something that's a surprise that they don't want you to see. But if you give me five minutes, I'll make sure that it's okay for you to come in."

He shook his head at me. "As it turns out, I'm meeting with someone who might know a bit more about that alchemy book. It's been puzzling me."

"The one with the pages that look fresh even though it's an old book?" I had felt the magic surrounding the book. We'd visited the collector in New Zealand who'd previously owned the book. But oddly, when Rafe asked her about the alchemy text, she claimed the book had never been hers. She was so insistent that he let the matter drop. I'd felt the magic on the book which Rafe had bought for his collection. It was definitely spellbound.

"Yes," he said.

"You're meeting tonight?"

"Mm. It's handy to know dons who like to stay up late."

I wondered if the don was another vampire but didn't pry. It was shocking how many Oxford dons were undead.

I was sorry Rafe wasn't coming to the knitting club, but the vamps couldn't work on my dress if he was there, and it was exciting to see the gown taking shape.

Rafe and I parted ways outside my shop, and I watched him walk away until he headed down Rook Lane and disappeared from view.

I was a little late for the meeting, so when I got there, they were already hard at work. Everybody had a piece of my wedding dress, and crochet hooks were flying so fast, I grew dizzy watching them.

Sylvia and Gran were talking quietly as I approached. I heard snatches of their conversation before they knew I was there.

"She could stay young forever," Gran said.

Sylvia nodded. "It would be better for Rafe if she didn't age."

I nearly turned around and ran before stopping myself. This was my beloved grandmother and someone I mostly considered a friend. I moved closer.

"You two aren't thinking about turning me into a vampire, are you?" I tried to make a joke of it, but I think the horror seeped through in my voice. I thought I'd been clear that I wasn't interested.

They both looked up at me, so genuinely surprised that I figured they didn't have some devious plan to turn me without my permission.

"Of course not, dear," Gran assured me. "We were talking about Karmen, the Wicked Witch of Wallingford. Her youthfulness is entirely unnatural. And she's definitely not a vampire."

My heart settled down to something closer to normal speed. This conversation I could get behind. "It is curious, isn't it?" I looked at Gran. "What do you think is going on?"

"It's strong magic and nothing I've ever seen before. Or she's an alchemist who's discovered the elixir of life."

I nodded. Gran had said the same things earlier. "Speaking of witches," I said softly, "Mom and Dad are in town."

"Are they?" Gran stopped crocheting to stare at me. Obviously, she and Sylvia hadn't checked their phones in the past couple of hours.

"Yes. And you know what that means."

Gran nodded. "Susan will be vulnerable to being taken

over by dark forces. Again. I do wish that stubborn daughter of mine would accept her powers."

Yeah, probably not going to happen. "It also means that you have to stay out of sight." I looked at her sternly. "No sneaking up into the back room to have a chat. No little walks into town."

She looked abashed. "You know about those." She sighed. "All right. I'll be more careful."

"I'm going back to Wallingford," Sylvia said as though the conversation hadn't moved on.

"Why?"

Sylvia glanced up at me and back to her work. "To persuade the too-young-for-her-years witch to share her secret. I shall go and see her again. It would be so nice for Rafe if he could count on you for longer than your mortal years."

I hadn't liked Karmen, but I didn't want her being "persuaded" to tell Sylvia her secrets. I'd seen Sylvia at her worst, and it wasn't anything I wanted to witness again. "You're not thinking of doing anything bad to her, are you?"

Sylvia sent me a cold stare. "Not unless giving someone a large sum of money is now considered in bad taste."

"Right." I would sit down and shut up before I got myself into any more trouble saying tactless things in a roomful of vampires.

I looked around at all the pieces of my wedding dress almost magically appearing. "What can I do to help?" My crochet was about as good as my knitting, but I had a selection of hooks with me. I could learn as I went.

Sylvia glanced over at me. "It's all right, dear. We have it all in hand."

"But I want to help," I said, my voice ending on a whine so I sounded like Hester the permanently petulant teenager. Though even Hester had a piece of my wedding dress to work on, and she looked smugly superior when she glanced my way.

"Couldn't I at least do some of the ribbing?" I knew what ribbing was. And I was pretty sure I could do it.

Sylvia gave an artificial-sounding titter. "Don't you know it's bad luck for the bride to work on her own dress?"

I'd never heard of any such thing. I shook my head at her. "No, it's not. It's bad luck for the groom to see the wedding dress before the wedding day." So not the same thing.

She glanced up at me and said, "Well, if you worked on this dress, it would be bad luck."

Twelve vampires made various hastily concealed sounds of amusement. I thought about acting like Hester and throwing a fit, but Sylvia was right. The dress would look a lot better if I didn't have a hand in it.

CHAPTER 5

*W*hen I arrived at the shop the next morning, Violet was there ahead of me looking sulky.

"Good morning," I said, wondering what was wrong.

"Morning. Did you have a nice time yesterday?"

Was she still irked about me leaving her for the afternoon?

I told her about the interesting crystal shop and the guy who was going to carve the moonstone buttons for me. She didn't seem terribly interested in my anecdote. Her face went more sour. We're talking sucking-lemons sour.

"You might have called to make sure everything was fine in the shop. But clearly you were too busy with your wedding plans to spare a thought for me stuck here all by myself on a Friday afternoon."

That stung. I said, "As a matter of fact, I was thinking about you yesterday. It might interest you to know that I found the witch who sold that hex. You remember, the one that had your hair falling out and your teeth falling out and your skin breaking out all over the place? The one I helped reverse?"

Okay, maybe I was being as childish as she was, reminding her that I'd all but saved her life, but I had a lot on my mind right now. Including what on earth I was going to do with my parents for the next two weeks until the wedding.

She slapped the wool she was pricing down on the counter. "Now I'm even more annoyed that you didn't give me a phone call. You found the witch that sold that hex?" She turned an astonished face my way. "The one that nearly killed me? And you didn't immediately tell me?"

"What could you have done about it? You were running the shop, as you keep reminding me. Anyway, if you want to see her so badly, her name is Karmen, and she lives in Wallingford."

I was a bit worried about the bridesmaid gift, so I tested Violet to see if she'd freak out when she found out who'd made her gift. "Karmen makes these fabulous skin creams." I leaned closer to her. "Don't you think my skin already looks better?" I'd spread some on my face this morning, and my cheeks felt smoother, I was convinced.

She squinted at me. "Not really. I wouldn't put anything on my face that witch touched. No doubt, instead of getting a dewy, youthful glow, my skin would turn as leathery and gray as an elephant's and slide off my face."

That was a horrifying image. I touched my own cheeks. "It feels really good. I think she infuses her creams with magic."

Violet sniffed. "I'm not sure I like that woman's magic. It's altogether too much on the dark end of the spectrum."

Maybe I'd have a rethink on the bridesmaid gifts.

Saturday mornings were always busy in the shop, so there were customers in and out, and I didn't get a chance to tell Violet about my mother being in town. Mrs. Darlington, one of my most regular customers, came in to buy wool for a lightweight spring sweater. It was so nice to see the spring colors, and I was happy to help her choose something that would be flattering for her daughter, who was about my age.

She left, and there was a lull. Quickly, before anyone else came in the shop, I told Violet that my mother and father had surprised me and were staying in Oxford until the wedding.

"That's nice," she said.

Was that sarcasm or not? Sometimes I couldn't tell with Violet. I decided not to inquire.

"The thing is, she wants to help you organize my hen party."

"But I don't need help to organize your hen party. I have it all under control." She tossed her black hair over her shoulder, and the ribbon of dyed pink seemed to shake a neon finger at me.

"Right. Because there isn't going to be a hen party," I reminded her. We'd definitely discussed this.

"Of course, there isn't." Too sincere. Was that more sarcasm?

"Good. So, when my mother asks to help organize it, you can be the one to tell her I'm not having one."

"Of course. Push all your dirty work onto me. As always."

This mood of hers was really getting under my skin. I was supposed to be a blushing bride full of orange blossoms and hazy dreams. Instead, I seemed to be dragged down by other people's bad moods. Sylvia was testy, Violet was being downright unpleasant, and even Nyx was acting up.

I had started packing up a few things, getting ready for my move into Rafe's manor house. I'd never met a cat who embraced change, and Nyx, familiar or not, was no different. She'd jumped into my packing boxes when I was in the middle of packing them and glared at me. I tried to explain to her that this was a good thing, and she'd be spending more time with her debatably second favorite person in the world, but I sometimes suspected she thought I was up to no good. She, like Violet, seemed to think that my marriage was entirely designed to make her life more miserable.

A narcissistic assistant I could probably deal with, but a narcissistic familiar? That had to be against the witchy rules.

A few minutes later, I was relieved that I'd warned Violet my mother was in town when Mom walked into the shop. She looked well-rested and full of plans. My mother has supervised the unearthing of entire dynasties of illustrious Egyptians and Syrians. When she is full of energy, my heart usually quails. I do not wish for my plans and my secrets to be dug up, dusted, investigated, and put on display. But, invariably, that's how my mother gets to work.

She was thrilled to see Violet and gave her a big hug. Then she glanced around the shop and shook her head. "It's funny. Every time I come here, this shop is smaller than I remember."

And amazingly, every time she said it, I still wanted to poke her in the belly with one of the knitting needles.

I restrained myself, of course, and had the pleasure of seeing Meri walk in.

"You remember Meri?" I said to Violet. Meri's not understanding technology had been a slight hindrance when she'd worked here, but she was so very pleasant, such a good knitter, and so good at serving people that she'd been in many ways a much better assistant than Violet.

While I took Meri around and showed her the few changes we'd made since she'd been there, and she ran her small hands over some of the new crochet cottons including a pretty shade of pale pink, I said, "Why don't you crochet yourself a sweater while you're here?" I smiled at her. "You still get the employee discount. That's as immortal as you are."

She giggled behind her hand. "I would like to make something pretty. I am as yet unaccustomed to your shops. It is much easier for me to craft my own garments." She sighed. "I will make something pretty to wear to your wedding."

I loved this plan. We pulled out some magazines and chose a pretty, lacy, short-sleeved sweater that I thought would look gorgeous on her. I told her I'd take her shopping before the wedding and choose a skirt to go with it. While we were doing this, Mom and Violet were chatting away like the best of friends. Okay, they were related, but our two families had not been close until recently. I was suspicious about what they had to talk about with such animation.

When I got back over to them, Mom said, "Violet and I have put our heads together about your hen party. You'll have to excuse Violet. I'm sneaking her away for a little while."

I raised my eyebrows and tried to skewer my wayward assistant with my coldest glance. She was impervious.

"I'll take an early lunch," Violet said.

"It's eleven o'clock," I protested.

"Oh nonsense, Vi," my mother said. "Lucy can do without you for the rest of the day. Besides, I'm sure Meri would love to catch up with Lucy, and she can assist in the shop if it gets busy." And wasn't that nice of my mother to take charge of my shop, my staffing, and drag Violet out to plan a hen party that I did not want. My day was turning out really well.

On the plus side, Meri was a pleasure to be around, and instead of constantly sniping at me, turned to me as though I had all the answers in the universe. It made for a refreshing change.

She said, "I am very happy to help in your beautiful shop. I have missed you and Cardinal Woolsey's."

It was so nice to have her back. "We've missed you. But I bet it's nice to be home."

"It is. Everything is so much more familiar to me in Egypt. Especially when I am unearthing those I have known in life."

I couldn't imagine. That must be weird. I said, "Don't worry about helping. Go sit in the visitor's chair and start on your sweater. If it gets busy, I'll call you."

She looked shocked. "I cannot sit at my leisure while you work. You make light of saving me from the prison in which I was trapped for two thousand years, but I am forever grateful. Please, you sit and let me work."

Well, this was never going to happen. For one thing, I couldn't crochet a sweater. I supposed I could make a start though. I said, "I tell you what. I'll bring another chair out, and we'll sit together. Maybe I'll make myself a sweater. Could you help me if I get stuck with the crochet?"

"It would be my pleasure." And so the two of us sat working away. The thing with crochet is at least there's only one hook and not two needles. And you can do things like squares and pieces that you sew together later. I know you can do that with knitting, too, but it seems more common with crochet. Anyway, I decided that I would crochet myself one of those pretty, short-sleeved sweaters in mint green. If Meri and I wore them together and stood side by side, no doubt we'd look like a couple of Easter eggs, but I couldn't imagine that would happen very often, if at all. And imagine Rafe's surprise when I showed up wearing a sweater that I'd actually made myself.

We worked away happily, and when a customer came in, either I would serve them or Meri would. It didn't seem to matter. It was a sunny day in Oxford, and everyone seemed to be in a good mood. Violet not being here was like a black cloud had wafted out the door.

No sooner had I had that thought than a very different and frankly darker black cloud wafted in the door. I felt a slight chill and looked up to find Margaret Twigg standing staring at the two of us crocheting away as though we were two kids skipping school and she was our strict teacher. But then, she always had that effect on me.

From her basket in the window, Nyx stood on all fours, arched her back and hissed. She was not fond of Margaret Twigg.

I put down my crochet and stood up. "Margaret, what are you doing here?" If I'd had more time to think, I would have said, "What a pleasure to see you," even though it wasn't. I was even annoyed at myself that I'd stood up. I should have remained sitting. It was my shop, after all. But, somehow, Margaret Twigg intimidated me so much that I'd rather stand up so at least we were somewhat on the same level.

As far as I knew, Margaret Twigg did not knit, so by process of elimination she was here on witch business.

"I haven't seen you since Beltane," she said. I could still

recall the ceremony and the fires as we witches welcomed spring.

"I've had a lot going on. Like planning a wedding."

She said, "I've come to talk to you about officiating at your wedding. Do you want a proper, traditional Wiccan ceremony?"

I felt as though my ears had suddenly blocked up with ice. What was all this about Margaret Twigg being our wedding officiant? It was the first I'd heard of it. And I was pretty certain Rafe wouldn't have asked her to take on such an important task without discussing it with me.

I swallowed. "Wedding officiant?" I asked as though I'd never heard the term before.

"Yes," she said, a touch impatient. "I need to know what sort of ceremony you want. Obviously, I'll be the one to marry you and Rafe. I am the head of your coven, after all."

"But don't you need to be a licensed Registrar?" I had done a bit of research. Bizarrely, a garden wedding wasn't legal. A marriage had to occur in a fixed building. But Margaret waved such details aside. "You'll have a short, legal ceremony at the registry office beforehand, and I'll perform the ceremony to celebrate your union."

Actually, that made a lot of sense. I was going to have to do better than this if I didn't want to have Margaret Twigg officiating at my wedding. If I wanted to turn and run in the middle of the ceremony, I wouldn't be able to. I'd have to say "I do" or risk the wrath of Margaret. Not that I wanted to run away from my own wedding. Just having her looking at me was giving me crazy thoughts.

"I hadn't—Rafe and I haven't—"

"Discuss it with him and let me know, but don't leave it too long. I'll have to make preparations."

I nodded, too confused to say a word.

She nodded briskly. "I'll let you get back to it. Good afternoon, Meritanum."

"Good afternoon."

Even the bells seemed to have a different sound when she shut the door on her way out. Almost as if they were giving out bell-like sighs of relief.

Meri said in a small voice, "That witch frightens me."

"That witch frightens me, too. And now it seems like she's going to be the one marrying me."

Meri giggled. "No. It is Rafe who will be marrying you. And that is something all of us who wish you well have wanted for a very long time."

When she put it like that, the actual ceremony didn't matter much at all.

I sat back down again and resumed my crochet. The nice thing about working with Meri was that she also moved her needle at a human pace. I felt less intimidated than with my usual knitting and crochet companions, who'd have had an entire sweater completed in the time it took me to knit—and then probably have to unpick—a single row.

Not long after that, Sylvia walked in from the street. She blinked when she saw Meri and then, recognizing her, went forward with her hands held out. "Meri. What a pleasure to see you here."

Meri was a great favorite with the vampires. She rose and returned Sylvia's embrace.

"Everyone will want to see you. Especially Agnes. Poor

Agnes, she feels so shut in knowing that her daughter is in town and she daren't be seen."

"That is very sad," Meri said.

"But seeing you will cheer her up. Why don't you come down tonight? It will be a surprise for Agnes and a very welcome one. You can spend the evening with us."

Meri looked up at me as though she needed my permission, and I nodded. "That's a great idea. And if it gets late, you can stay in the guest room upstairs."

She nodded. "I would be most honored." Then she looked down and blushed. "But Pete will come and fetch me."

Sylvia chuckled. "And Pete is fetching you, is he? Well, well. I suppose one saw that coming. We'll be making another wedding gown soon, I imagine."

Meri was the color of her crochet cotton. "He has not spoken. Please. I do not know—"

"Stop embarrassing her," I said to Sylvia. When I saw the way Pete looked at Meri, I suspected Sylvia was correct, but we should let them figure out their plans first. Not that the vampires excelled at staying out of other people's business, as I knew only too well.

"I am most grateful and honored by your kind invitation," Meri said again.

"It's so nice to see a young woman with such good manners," Sylvia said.

And then, with a slight glance at me, she headed into the back room. I didn't know if she was trying to intimate that I didn't have good manners or that she would quite like it if I was a little more servile. That was not going to happen.

~

I WAS ABOUT to close up shop when my mother returned, alone. She said, "Oh, we had a delightful afternoon. She's such a lovely girl, Violet."

"She is. Also, a very good shop assistant."

My sarcastic barb went wide. The door opened again, and if I'd thought it might be my wayward assistant here to help close, I was wrong. It was my dad, looking very pleased with himself. "I've had a marvelous afternoon at the Ashmolean. Met up with Hughes. Been talking about a joint project. It could be very exciting."

"That's great, Dad." Professor Hughes had gone to school with my dad and written a few books that had quoted my parents. I'd much rather talk about Egyptology with my folks than my wedding.

My mother, however, was not to be so easily distracted. And usually Mom was as obsessed as my dad with their work.

She said, "That's wonderful, Jack. And you can tell me all about it later. But your father and I were speaking last night, Lucy, and we've decided to sell our home in Boston."

"Sell the family home?" This came out of nowhere.

Dad was looking pleased, and Mom continued, "We talked it over, and really we were keeping it in case you needed a place to go when things didn't work out."

Oh, didn't I sound like a winner in their eyes. Had they really kept the house in case I needed a bolt hole?

"Where will you live?"

They glanced at each other. "We think we'll come here when we retire so we can be nearer to our only daughter."

Okay, I could see that was going to be fraught with problems, but I'd cross that bridge...

My dad entered the discussion. "We've put by a nice sum for when you got married, but I spoke to Rafe, and he says the wedding will cost next to nothing, seeing as it's being held at his house and catered by his staff. He refused our money, so we thought we'd add it to the house money and buy something nice here."

My mother nodded. "We almost spent your wedding money on a new car. After you and Todd broke up, it didn't seem likely that we'd be called upon to pay for a wedding." They both chuckled as though this were a humorous anecdote.

I was long over the humiliation of Todd's betrayal, but nobody likes to be reminded of that day their boyfriend butt-dialed them while engaging in amorous activities with somebody else.

"First, however, we've got your hen party to think about. Violet and I had such fun planning it." Her eyes twinkled. I hadn't seen Mom that excited since she dug up a jeweled bracelet that could have belonged to Cleopatra.

Clearly, I hadn't managed to impress upon Vi how very much I did not want this. I turned to Mom. "Please, I don't want to be paraded through the streets of Oxford on some drunken pub crawl."

"Nonsense. It's a rite of passage, my love. Don't worry. We'll be there to hold you up if you get tipsy." So not the maternal support I'd been hoping for.

I wanted to argue more, but Dad grabbed my mother's arm. "Come on, Susan. We've got drinks with Professor Pinkerton and her husband. Mustn't keep them waiting."

Mom glanced at her watch. "Right. Never a dull moment." And with a wave, she and my dad were off.

CHAPTER 6

Sunday morning found me at Rafe's place. We were enjoying a lazy morning which seemed more than usually luxurious as I'd been so busy recently. William made me brunch—eggs Florentine with homemade cheese scones. So good. While I ate, I told Rafe about my dread over my hen night and my mother's insistence on this embarrassing ritual.

"Poor you," he said, looking slightly appalled.

I put extra butter on my scone. Not that I needed it, but I had no willpower where William's cooking was concerned. "I relied on Violet to stop her, but Vi's as bad. How am I going to get out of this?"

"I'm not sure you can. It's only one night, and if it gets too much, text me and I'll spirit you away."

"Unless you're underneath a lap dancer at the time," I muttered.

"I beg your pardon?"

"My father's got plans, too, you know. For you."

"I'll have Lochlan put a stop to that. All the wedding planning seems to be precipitously early."

He was right. Even Jennifer, my oldest friend, had decided to make a holiday of it and was arriving tomorrow. She was a fan of the exclamation mark at the best of times. When she was excited, there were more punctuation marks than letters.

"Hey Loose!!!!!!!!!!" her most recent email had started.

"Sick news!!!!!!! I got extra time off work and I'm headed your way!!!!!!!!!!!!!!!!! Can't wait to catch up, see Oxford and meet the fiancé!!!!!!!!!!!! Can't believe you found your lobster first!!!!!!!!!!!!!!!!!!!!!!"

I had to smile that she'd used a *Friends* reference. We'd watched all ten seasons together.

I'd tried to explain it to Rafe, but he had no idea who Ross and Rachel were or why anyone would be interested in them. The lobster thing was a step too far. I could imagine him looking at me, all cool and intellectual, and saying, "But that's absurd. Lobsters don't mate for life. They're not even monogamous."

I didn't even try.

Apart from his lack of modern culture, Rafe was an excellent companion, and we chatted about his work, my work, the wedding, the future. Now that I'd accepted my feelings for him and his proposal, we were free to share everything, knowing we'd be part of each other's lives until death did us part. Mine, most likely, but I pushed that thought away.

When William returned to clear my all-but-licked-clean plate, he brought in a wrapped gift. "This came for you both by private courier."

"Ooh, a present," I squealed.

Rafe looked amused. "You're like a small child at Christmas."

"I don't care what you think. I love presents."

"Then you'd better open it."

I pulled the silver ribbon away and happily tore into the white and silver paper. Inside was a white cardboard box. I removed the lid and peeked inside.

I saw something wooden that appeared old. Gingerly, I lifted out a box with strange symbols carved into it. I thought at first the writing was Egyptian hieroglyphics, which I could read, having spent many a summer helping my parents on digs. However, while the symbols were similar, they weren't Egyptian.

I showed Rafe, who accepted the box and studied the inscription. "These are runes," he said. "Very old. I wonder if this is from Lochlan." He glanced around. "Was there a card?"

I'd been so eager to unwrap the present, I hadn't even looked for a card. Now we searched, but there wasn't any indication who the gift had come from. "Open the box," I said. "Maybe there's a card inside."

Sometimes I'm not so smart.

He lifted the lid, and an odd expression crossed his face.

"What is it?" I leaned forward to look. Then pulled my head sharply back again. "Ugh. It looks like camel dung that's been petrified." That might sound like an odd thing to say, but I'd spent enough summers in Egypt that I knew what petrified camel dung looked like. Like a baked potato in its jacket left in the oven too long. "Why would Lochlan send us camel dung?"

"I don't think it is from Lochlan, and it's not camel dung."

He put two fingers into the box and retrieved a note. "'To Lucy, from an admirer,'" he read aloud. "And there are instructions. 'Break off a little of this mixture, stir it into wine and drink it. To be repeated as needed. Excellent for a youthful complexion. No expiry date.'"

It didn't look like anything I wanted to put in my mouth. I leaned closer and sniffed it gingerly. There was a slightly familiar scent to it, like a memory I couldn't quite catch. Until I did.

"What do the runes say?" If he couldn't read them, he was exactly the man to have the right research books to figure out the message. It was no surprise when he picked up the box and studied the runes. "It translates roughly into 'As above, so below.'"

"That's an alchemical saying, isn't it?"

"Yes."

Rafe said, "Alchemy is about combining opposite elements to make something very special. As above, so below, male with female, light with darkness, day with night."

"You with me," I said and he smiled.

"The metaphor holds."

"Why would someone send a wedding gift that's only for you?" William asked, looking puzzled. He'd stayed to see us open the present. He was like me and loved gifts. Though maybe not this one.

"I think the part that's for Rafe is if I drink this stuff, it'll keep me looking young." I hadn't planned to tell them about the witch who seemed not to age, but someone had forced my hand. Now I told them about meeting the Wicked Witch of Wallingford.

"Why would the witch give you her closely guarded secret recipe?" William wanted to know.

I shook my head slowly. "I don't know. The whole thing

doesn't make sense. She knows I'm getting married, but she didn't seem the type to share her secrets. I don't trust her."

Rafe pulled the box away from me. "Please don't ingest any of this until I've had it tested."

What did he think I was, stupid? "I'm not eating that stuff." I felt queasy just thinking about it.

"How about coffee on the terrace?" William suggested. Oh, he was good. A change of scene and a coffee would definitely help settle me.

"Olivia's got some ideas for floral arrangements she wants to discuss with you. I'll send her out to you, shall I?"

"Perfect."

"I'll join you out there in a moment," Rafe said, picking up the rune box and taking it down the hall toward his study. Good.

"WILLIAM!" I called out Sunday afternoon. "William!"

"What are you bellowing about?" Rafe asked from behind his newspaper. Rafe wasn't one to grab his news from an iPhone app. He still had a broadsheet delivered every morning.

"I need stuff."

"What stuff?"

"Well, cardboard. Colored felt pens. Stuff like that."

He looked at me, fascinated. "Might one inquire why?"

"Yes, one might. I want to make a sign with Jennifer's name on it for when I get to the airport. I'm picking her up tomorrow." I felt a sudden longing to see my childhood friend. "I can't wait."

He looked at me as though I might be running a fever. "Did you not tell me that this woman has been your best friend your whole life? And yet you need to hold up a sign with her name on it so you recognize each other?"

I rolled my eyes. "It's a joke. A fun thing. I haven't seen her for two years." I turned to him. "You know how celebrities and important people always have a driver standing, waiting with a sign for them at Heathrow. I thought it would be fun to do it for Jennifer."

"I see." And he retreated back behind his paper.

There was a reason I hadn't asked Rafe for help. I kept going toward the kitchen. "William."

I found William muttering to himself over tiny rounds of puff pastry. "Taste these, Lucy. I'm not at all sure. I'm experimenting. These would be passed around on trays during your wedding reception. I want everything to be perfect." We'd decided on this style of food so it wouldn't be obvious that the vampires weren't eating, as it would if we had a sit-down meal. There would also be a buffet table set up with more hearty fare.

"Everything will be perfect, William." However, I wasn't above grabbing the small savory just to check and see. I popped it in my mouth, chewed and closed my eyes in bliss. "William, that is fantastic."

"You're sure, Lucy? The mushroom flavor's not too strong?"

"The mushroom flavor is spectacular. Honestly, you'll get tension headaches or an ulcer or something if you don't relax."

"I want everything to be perfect. For both of you."

I had one of those all too frequent washes of emotion that

misted my eyes. I threw my arms around William from the back and rested my cheek between his shoulder blades. "Thank you. I know it's not going to be easy, but the future will be so much better knowing that you're part of it."

He turned, and I caught a worried expression on his face. "Are you sure, Lucy? I know you're not accustomed to managing servants. Olivia and I will do everything we can to make your lives run smoothly, but if it's too much, perhaps—."

"You're not servants. Not to me. I feel like we're family. A team."

He brightened up at that. "That's a very nice way to put it. Thank you."

I said, "And as part of that team, could you find me some cardboard and colored markers? Sparkles? Sequins? Fake jewels if you have them?"

He blinked at me. "Are you planning to star in a burlesque show?"

Oh, very funny. "No." Again I explained my plan. Unlike Rafe, William had a chuckle and thought Jennifer would enjoy being met by somebody holding a welcome sign. By digging through drawers and raiding Rafe's office, but most especially going through all William's catering supplies, we found all kinds of fun things. He even helped me. "This is all left over from a child's birthday party I catered," he said, dragging down a plastic tub. "And this is from a golden wedding." He dragged down another.

As I glued plastic balloons from the kids' party onto a big piece of pasteboard I'd covered in bright pink fabric, I said, "If I'd had time, I'd have asked Theodore to make this. But it's more fun if I do it myself." I pulled out a plastic tiara covered in jewels. "What do you think? Stick the tiara on top? Or pull off the jewels and stick them on separately?"

He picked up the tiara and set it on top of my sign. "I'd attach it to the sign, and when she joins you, make her wear it out of the airport."

I burst out laughing. "Brilliant."

He pulled out a second tiara and set it on my head. "You'd best wear one yourself, too."

It didn't take us too long and we had a beautiful sign. Jennifer's name sparkled with sequins, and the sign was dotted with rhinestones, and Olivia found me a stick that we stapled the sign to so that I could hold it up. Very professional. I was practically jumping up and down on Monday morning when it was time to leave for the airport.

Rafe said, "Are you sure you don't want me to drive you, Lucy?"

I shook my head firmly. "I'll be fine." The truth was I didn't love driving in England, and I'd never actually navigated my way in and out of Heathrow, but how hard could it be? Besides, Jennifer and I needed some alone time. Some catching-up girl time. To that end, I'd told Violet that I was going to be late arriving at the shop. She'd heaved a huge sigh of discontent, but I was getting used to those.

I slipped into a pretty spring sweater in pale blue that Alfred had knit for me and wore it over cream trousers. Then I set out for Heathrow with Rafe reminding me yet again to call immediately if I had any problems.

I walked over and kissed him. "What will you do while I'm gone?"

"I'm still trying to make head or tail of that alchemy book. Something about it is bothering me."

"Probably the spell. Look, when I get some time, I'll take a look at it too. Between us, maybe we'll figure out what to do with it. Or who it belongs to."

I think that was my biggest worry. What if some witch/alchemist had misplaced this and needed it back? I knew how I'd feel if my grimoire went missing. Maybe I didn't study it as diligently as I should, but it was always there. If I needed a spell, I knew where to go. It was part of my bloodline. Part of my heritage. I wondered if this was the heritage of someone else and they were frantically searching. It had come to Rafe in a mysterious fashion, after all. The New Zealand collector claimed not to have sold it to him. So who had? And why?

Book collecting wasn't particularly secretive, but the intermediary seller had disappeared when Rafe tried to contact them.

I couldn't worry about that now. I had my best friend to pick up at the airport. My best friend and bridesmaid. Sometimes I'd catch myself glancing at my engagement ring just to see it sitting there on my finger announcing my news to all the world.

I got in my little red car, then got out again, as Henri the peacock had waddled up and stood behind my car, clearly waiting to be fed. I got out and scolded him while simultaneously giving him a treat. The bird didn't seem to notice the mixed messaging. He was clearly only receiving the message that had the treat in it. Then he waddled off quite happily, and I got back in the car one more time.

In good traffic, it was about an hour and a quarter to the airport. I gave myself two hours to account for traffic and any wrong turns I might make. I headed down on the A40, played

Billie Eilish, and tried to control my excitement. Now that almost everyone was here, this wedding was getting real.

Maybe it was the rhythmic driving or the music taking up one part of my brain and leaving some other part of it free, but I started to think about that spellbound alchemy book. I wondered if I was right and the reason Rafe wasn't getting anywhere was because he wasn't a witch. The New Zealand collection had been amazing, if you went in for old books, but there were no grimoires, no alchemy texts. I believed the collector when she said that alchemy book hadn't come from her. Where, then, had it come from?

And what about that strange gift in the rune box? Sylvia had said she might go back and try to get Karmen to sell her the secret formula to her youthful appearance. Had she? And if so, why hadn't she signed her name to the note? That must have been a very expensive gift, and Sylvia wasn't one to hide her good deeds.

By concentrating hard, I managed to get to the right terminal and breathed a sigh of relief when I parked the car. I grabbed my homemade sign and tiara, ignored the surprised glances that people shot me as they saw my garish placard, and made my way into the terminal. I went up near the big exit doors where Jennifer would come out and took up my position.

I wasn't the only person standing there holding a sign with someone's name on it, but I was definitely the only one that had prettied up their sign. Among the dark-suited, serious drivers holding papers and cardboard up with person or persons' names in black felt pen, I felt that my limousine service was head and shoulders above theirs in the wow factor. No one else was greeting their ride customer while wearing a tiara.

The plane was on time, but even so, it was probably half an hour before Jennifer came out.

I caught sight of her before she saw me. Her dark hair had grown longer. Otherwise, she looked the same as always. Her brown eyes lit up when she saw me, and she threw back her head and laughed. It was the kind of laugh, big and brimming with personality, that made other people turn and stare. She pushed her cart loaded with luggage towards me, and when she got around the barrier, I ran to her and threw my arms around her, squealing.

"Jen!" I cried. "It's so good to see you."

"And to think I was worried I wouldn't recognize you," she said, hugging me back. "Two years. I haven't seen you for two years."

"I know. We have so much to catch up on."

Before she did anything else, she grabbed my hand and stared at the engagement ring. "That is beautiful," she said. "I can't wait to see the groom. I'm still mad at you that you never sent me any pictures of him."

"He hates cameras. It's a weird personality thing. Otherwise, he's semi-normal."

As I settled her plastic tiara on her head she said, "If he's marrying you, he can't be very normal."

I chuckled. She was right there.

We pushed her trolley to the car park and unloaded the bags into my car. "Are you moving to the UK?" I asked. There were some heavy suitcases here.

"I wasn't sure what I'd need. Everyone says the weather in England can be unpredictable this time of year, so I pretty much brought my whole wardrobe. My best girl's getting married. I'm taking a vacation."

"I think that's a great idea."

She naturally walked towards the driver's side, as every North American does, and then giggled and re-routed herself to the passenger side.

I told her I couldn't talk until I'd navigated my way out of Heathrow. She yawned and obligingly kept her mouth shut until I'd managed to get all the way out of Heathrow and headed in the correct direction back towards Oxford. Then I said, "Okay, tell me everything."

"Well, everybody sends their best wishes and is super jealous that I got invited to your wedding and they didn't."

I winced slightly. "We're trying to keep the wedding small. Besides, I didn't want people to have to pay a lot of money to come and see me get married."

"That's okay. Everybody understands." She leaned towards me until our shoulders bumped. "I saw the Toad."

I did a theatrical grimace and shudder combination. My cheating ex, Todd, would forever be the Toad to Jen and me. "I hope you told him I was getting married." I might not care about him anymore, but I wanted to rub his nose in my happiness on principle.

"Babe, I've got your back. I not only told him you were getting married, I told him you were marrying a guy with a title and a castle."

I burst out laughing. The crazy thing was, it was true. Rafe never used his title, but William had shown me the documents. He was Sir Rafe Crosyer, knighted by Queen Elizabeth herself. The first one.

"And what's the Toad doing?" I asked. I didn't really care, but I could tell she wanted to share.

"Well, he got downsized from his job. Because he's an idiot. Monica and he got back together, but that'll never last. Basically, he's the same."

"Did he send me a message or anything?"

"You know Todd. He said, 'Some chicks get all the breaks.'"

Then we talked more about mutual friends, though I could see those friendships already fading after two years. She said, "When are you coming home? Even just for a visit?"

"Honestly, I don't know. I'm sure I'll take Rafe back to show him where I grew up, but I like it here. My life is here now. I can't wait for you to see my little shop. I'm learning to knit."

"So you keep saying. Are you any good?"

"Absolutely terrible."

She burst out laughing. "I learned to knit."

"No way."

"I did. When we were all stuck staying home anyway, I learned it by watching videos online."

"Are you any good?"

"Not bad. I knitted a few scarves, and then I tried socks. Socks are harder than you'd think."

If Jen could successfully knit socks, she was way ahead of me.

"When are your parents arriving?"

"They're already here. They're very excited to see you."

"Wow. It seems ages." She turned to me. "Do you know we're going to be thirty this year?"

"I had noticed that. Yes."

I would be first, on the twenty-first of June. Jennifer was a September baby. She said, "I sort of thought I'd be married by now or at least know what I was doing."

"You're doing great."

"No. I'm really not." A lorry, aka a truck, overtook me and then cut in front of me. I was in the slow lane, but apparently going at the speed limit was too slow for some drivers. Jen took off her tiara and played with it in her lap. "I quit my job."

Okay, this was a surprise. "You did?"

"I was bored and not going anywhere. Well, you remember what it's like working in a cubicle all day?"

I nodded, so happy I never had to go back. Working in a knitting shop wasn't always ideal, but it suited me much better than a corporate career. "But you got that promotion." I remembered how excited she'd been.

"I did. I think that was the beginning of the end. Working in the medical insurance field isn't my dream job, and then I had to hire and motivate people, and I couldn't do it anymore." I felt the intensity of her stare, though I didn't want to shift my eyes from the road even for a second. "We're going to be thirty! I need to find my career before it's too late."

"Okay," I said. "You're smart, personable. You'll find the right thing."

"If only I knew what it was. I've always admired people who grow up knowing they want to be a doctor or astronaut or whatever. I still don't know."

"We'll figure it out. I'll help you."

"Single, jobless, and thirty. Never saw that coming."

Why did I suddenly feel guilty? I was marrying the love of my life, loved my job, and so turning thirty wasn't any more traumatic than knowing my youth was fading. I completely understood how Jen felt, though. "What happened with Brandon? You never said."

"Nothing happened with Brandon. We'd have drifted on forever if I hadn't broken up with him. I checked the girl-friend box for him and he checked the boyfriend box for me, but it wasn't going anywhere." She shifted in her seat. "Maybe I'll meet a great guy at your wedding."

Oh, she'd meet lots of great guys, but most of them would be undead.

CHAPTER 7

As we drove into Oxford, Jennifer cried out with delight. "Oh my God. I've seen these buildings in like a million movies." It was great fun to see her excitement, and I took a little pride in being able to tell her a bit about the colleges, point out the Radcliffe Observatory, the Bodleian, the Sheldonian. I was becoming a local.

She twisted around in her seat, taking everything in.

"This is really a walking city. I'll take you on a proper tour tomorrow. But for now, I thought I'd take you to the shop and we'd get you settled upstairs in my flat."

"You're sure you don't mind me staying with you? You must have so many friends and relatives that I can find a hotel."

We'd had this argument online. "No. You're staying with me. It'll be like a two-week slumber party."

She beamed at me. "I can't wait." We drove past a group of students. "I can't believe you live in Oxford. Do you feel smarter?"

"No. Mostly I feel like I don't know anything. Honestly,

just eavesdropping on kids' conversations on the street is intimidating. Most of the time I don't know what they're talking about. It's kind of fun, though."

I pulled onto Harrington Street and then down the narrow lane that led round to the back of the shop where I could park.

"And here we are," I said.

"It's so cute," she said, looking at the small herb garden that I really needed to tend.

We hauled her suitcases out of the back and then up the path to the door that led up to my flat.

"This is so nice," she said, when we reached the living room. She ran to look out of the window onto the street below. "The shop's downstairs," I told her, pointing to the set of stairs that led down to Cardinal Woolsey's. However, we took the stairs up one more level to the bedrooms. I showed Jen the bathroom and the guest room. She looked out of the bedroom window and squealed with excitement. "I can see the dreaming spires." She turned to me. "I can't wait to explore."

It was nice to have a guest who was enthusiastic. I felt proud of my adopted city.

"I should go check in at Cardinal Woolsey's. Why don't you unpack, make yourself at home, have a nap if you want to or a shower. Are you hungry? Because I've got some light snacks in the fridge."

"I ate on the plane, but I could sure use a cup of coffee and a shower."

"I'll put the coffee on. You shower. Walk on down to the shop when you're ready."

After I'd made coffee, I left Jen unpacking in the guest room.

I got back to the shop to find my cousin Violet in a particularly grumpy mood. She bit my head off when I said hi and complained that the shop was too hot and stuffy and that we should put in air-conditioning. She was right. It did sometimes get a little hot in there, but warm weather never lasted. And besides, I wasn't sure the old electric system could support air-conditioning. I thought it was something else making my cousin hot under the collar.

I tried to remain cheerful. I had my best friend here, after all. But I couldn't stop thinking about that box with the substance in it. "I can't think about that right now. I got a strange wedding gift. It looked like petrified dung in a box. I'm pretty sure it's from the Wicked Witch of Wallingford, but there wasn't even a proper card."

Vi looked horrified. "She's not invited to your wedding, is she?"

"No."

"Good. I think you should stay away from her. She's a troublemaker. And she tried to kill me, don't forget."

"I'll never forget that," I assured her. What an unpleasant time the hex had caused all of us.

We had a few customers, and then Alice popped in. She didn't work full time in Frogg's Books, but she was often to be found there. She and her husband, Charlie, were so happy, it was enough to make anybody believe in marriage.

She came in like a burst of fresh air and said, "Lucy, Violet, I'm so glad to have you together. I've got such news."

I didn't need my witch powers to divine her news before she

spilled it. There was a glow about Alice that made her beautiful. I could tell Violet had picked it up too, because her negative energy dipped even lower. It was like standing beside a black hole. I stepped forward as though I could shield poor Alice from Violet's dissatisfaction with life. I wouldn't spoil her surprise.

"What is it?" I asked, all innocent.

She made a movement as though she were jumping up and down without lifting her feet. Kind of like a bobbing doll. It was absolutely adorable. "I'm expecting."

My delight was sincere as I threw my arms around her and gave her a hug. "Congratulations. You'll be a wonderful mother."

"It's early days yet, so please don't tell anyone, but I had to let you know. I'm worried about my matron of honor dress. I think we might have to get something in stretchy fabric." She blushed adorably and put her hands to her still very flat stomach. "In case I'm showing."

I doubted very much she'd be showing in a couple of weeks, but I loved that she had shared her news with us. Violet finally managed to move forward, though she might as well have had heavy bricks instead of feet.

"That's great, Alice. I hope you'll be very happy," she managed. She sounded like she was giving a eulogy at a funeral, but she was doing her best.

Alice sent her a slightly surprised glance. "Thank you, Vi." Then she asked, "And when are we going shopping for bridesmaids' gowns?" She turned to me. "And what about your wedding dress? You haven't said. Don't tell me you've picked one out without us."

I was so thrilled that she cared enough to worry about my

dress. "Some friends are making it for me, as my wedding gift."

"Why, that's wonderful. What fabric have you chosen? I remember being torn between the silk and the chiffon and lace for the bodice." Her wedding hadn't been that long ago, and she still rhapsodized about a day that contained some challenges but led to a genuinely happy marriage. I shook my head, glad I hadn't had to make all those decisions.

"You mustn't tell anyone, because it's a surprise. But it's going to be made with crochet. Fine silk thread crocheted."

Her eyes opened wide. "What an enormous amount of work. Your friends will be working night and day."

Night, anyway.

"My friend Jennifer just arrived this morning. Let's give her a couple of days to get settled and then go shopping for dresses."

Two customers came in, and so she said, "I'd better get back."

"Saturday," I called after her. "Scarlett and Polly can take over the shop on Saturday so we can go shopping."

"And thank you so much for checking my schedule," Vi muttered darkly.

I turned to her, trying to be patient. "Would you be available on Saturday, Vi?"

She looked even more annoyed now. "I suppose so."

I told Alice we'd get together later to make final plans and then turned to my customers. I suggested to Violet that she might like to go into the back and pack some of the mail orders that were waiting. The more I could keep her away from the customers, the better my business was likely to do today.

One of my customers was an excited new grandmother. "The best part is it's twins, a boy and a girl, so no need to choose between pink and blue sweaters. I can make one of each."

The other was making slipper socks for her husband. "It's for his gout, you see. He likes the extra warmth."

Once I'd helped them choose wools and patterns and they'd left, I went into the back room, where Violet was packing packages with such violence, I was glad that wool wasn't breakable.

"Do you want to talk about whatever's bothering you?" I asked her.

She chucked the whole package down and slumped into a chair. This being England and all, I put the kettle on.

"I don't mean to be horrible, but you don't know what it's like. You're all happy and smelling of honeysuckle and bridal bouquets, and now Alice is having a baby, and I can't even get a date." With that, she burst into tears.

"I know it's hard. You just haven't met the right guy." It was such a feeble thing to say, but what else could I give her? It wasn't that she didn't try. She'd been on Witch Date, and that hadn't gone so well, dated several men who had turned out not to be the one. But worse, she had a close and friendly relationship with William Thresher, and I suspected she wanted more.

She wiped her wet cheeks with her hand. "What if I have met the right man? And he doesn't want me." Her voice wobbled at the end.

I wasn't going to beat around the bush anymore. "Is it William?"

She sniffed. "You know it is."

And, of course, I did.

"What's going on with you two? You seem to get on really well. He always asks you to help him when he has his catering gigs."

"I know. And sometimes he looks at me and I really think he might be interested. But he never makes a move or asks me out. I couldn't drop heavier hints. I'll say things like, 'I'll be alone Saturday night. Wonder what I'll watch on telly.'"

"Well, that sounds encouraging," I said.

"And then you know what he'll say to me? 'If I get a catering job on Saturday, I'll be sure to let you know.'"

Ouch. I thought about it for a minute. "Maybe he's just shy."

"And maybe he doesn't like me in that way." She was really having a pity party now.

"Do you think maybe it's time you found out once and for all?"

She sniffed again but looked up at me hopefully. "What do you mean? Some kind of revealing spell?"

"No. Not witchcraft. Actual, real, human communication. Why don't you ask him out?"

She put a hand to her forehead and looked as though she might faint with horror. "Sometimes you're so American."

Like that was a bad thing.

"At least talk to him. Tell him how you feel."

"No," she wailed. "I can't talk to William. It's hopeless. What if I asked him to go out and he said no? Then I wouldn't even be able to work with him anymore." She shook her head, and I thought she was getting more upset, not less, thanks to my little pep talk. "No, Lucy. I must accept it. I'll be a lone witch forever. One of those old crones that children are frightened of, in a tumbledown stone cottage in the middle of nowhere."

I immediately thought of Margaret Twigg, who lived in a stone cottage on the edge of Wychwood Forest. Though no one would consider Margaret lonely or pathetic. She was powerful and seemed more than happy with her single state. But Violet wasn't like that. And the more I thought about it, the more I believed she would make a good mate for William. She knew Rafe's secret, and being a witch, she had some secrets of her own.

She said, "I thought at least I might be paired with him in the wedding party. You know what they always say, if you're a bridesmaid, weddings are a great place to meet blokes. But he's not even in the wedding party," she wailed.

I'd been surprised by this too. "I don't think it's because he didn't want to walk down the aisle with you, Violet. William's the caterer. He didn't feel like he could both run the event and take part in it."

"I don't know. Personally, I think he ducked out of the wedding party to avoid me. No doubt he'll hire a load of pretty young things as waitresses to giggle and flirt with in the kitchen while I'm standing out there alone watching my cousin"—and here she glared at me—"my younger cousin get married."

I really did feel sorry for her, but this was getting old. I said, "I really think you should talk to him. You'll never know until you do."

JENNIFER DIDN'T COME DOWN to the shop, so I assumed she'd fallen asleep upstairs. Violet's mood had improved somewhat, so I felt safe leaving customers in her hands while I went to check on Jennifer. I went quietly up the stairs so as not to wake her and was surprised to find her sitting in my living room. "Jennifer? Everything okay?"

She glanced up at me with a funny look on her face. Then I looked around and understood her strange expression.

"Where did you get those?" I thought I'd hidden my witch paraphernalia so well. But she was sitting with my grimoire, my scrying mirror, and some black and white candles in front of her.

I had a cold, sick feeling in the pit of my stomach, probably what innocent young women in Salem felt when there was a certain knock on the door. I don't know why I was so nervous. It wasn't like they did terrible things to witches anymore, but I don't know, my craft was private. A part of my life I didn't readily share with people who didn't have magic. Jennifer and I had been friends for so long, I didn't know how she'd take this change in me. I couldn't bear to think I might lose my best friend over magic.

She touched the scrying mirror with her fingers, and the surface rippled like the surface of a pond in a breeze. There was no way I could pretend it wasn't what it was.

All she said was, "I wondered."

Since she obviously wasn't going to freak out and run screaming into Harrington Street, I walked closer and sat down beside her.

"What do you mean, you wondered? Did I act strange my whole life?" We seemed to be halfway into a conversation rather than beginning at the beginning.

"Remember when we used to play with the Ouija board?"

I'd almost forgotten. There'd been a stage when we were, I don't know, ten, eleven, twelve, when we'd run home from school and get out this old cardboard Ouija board that her mom had in the back of the closet. We'd both put our fingertips on the plastic planchette, ask questions, and the disk would fly around the board. Some of the answers we got were frighteningly accurate. I nodded.

"Remember when we asked about my uncle Pat, who was having tests in the hospital? And it spelled out D-E-A-D?"

I could never forget that moment. Jennifer's family didn't get the news until later that day. I nodded mutely.

"Didn't you ever wonder where we were getting that stuff from?"

I hadn't until now. "You think I was using my powers and didn't even know it?"

She smiled at me, put out her hand towards the grimoire, and to my absolute shock, as she raised her hand, the grimoire rose with it. She set it down and, with a practiced gesture, pointed at the candles, which immediately sprang into flame.

"You too? You're a witch?"

She nodded. "I always thought of you as a sister. Now I know you really are one."

I felt misty-eyed one more time. "How long have you known?"

"Not that long. I mean, I used to do things or think something might happen and then it would. But I didn't know I was special until after you left. I guess I was bored and missing my best friend. For something to do, I took a class in healing plants. The woman who gave the class was a witch who recognized my gift and mentored me."

"And you never said a word to me."

"You never shared your special talents with me, either."

Happiness rippled through me. Now I didn't have to keep this huge secret from one of my favorite people in the world. Instead of separating us, our magic bonded us. "It was so hard because we were far away. If we'd still been living near each other, of course I would have told you."

She looked at me seriously. "If we'd both been living the same lives, I bet we never would have discovered we were witches."

I shivered, thinking of missing out on my gift.

"Do you think that's why we were drawn together as kids?"

"Who knows? I'm glad we were, though."

"Me too."

I took her on the promised walking tour of Oxford, and then, that evening, we sat in my flat and talked for hours, catching up on old friends and reminiscing but mostly talking about magic. She got out her knitting, and I got back to work on my crocheted sweater. "Do you ever use magic to make your knitting go faster?" I asked her.

"No. It would take the fun away." She glanced up at me. "Do you?"

I shook my head. "Feels like cheating. Though I do have a spell for untangling wool that's very handy. Oh, and I've used a tidying-up spell in the shop."

"Completely understandable. That's like using a computer to write a letter instead of laboriously writing one by hand."

"Exactly. There's a time and place for everything."

Glad we understood each other, I suggested she might like to come to our next gathering of the coven.

"First, when do I get to meet the mysterious Rafe?"

"Tomorrow. He's invited us for lunch."

CHAPTER 8

"*a*bout time. I finally get to meet this groom of yours."
And then she poked a finger at me, mock-serious.
"And I'd better like him."

I felt strangely nervous about this meeting. Two people I
loved were going to meet, and I really wanted them to like
each other. What if they didn't? I wasn't going to cancel my
engagement because my bestie didn't like my fiancé, but I'd
be sad.

One thing I swore to myself. I wasn't going to magic her
into liking him. She'd take him on his own terms. Should I
tell her how very special he was? Even as the idea presented
itself, I rejected it. It was one thing to know that I was a witch,
something she could understand, since we shared that. But to
give away that I was marrying a vampire? That might be a
step too far. At least for now.

Next morning, I took Jen downstairs and showed her
around the shop, which took about five minutes, and introduced her to Violet. I wouldn't say the two clicked immediately, but Violet was polite and Jen enthusiastic about the

shop, the wedding and our Saturday excursion to buy brides-maid gowns.

Luckily, Scarlett had the day off from school, so she was helping in the shop. I'd done my best to schedule lots of help for Violet since I knew very well that I wouldn't be around very much for the next couple of weeks, and then Rafe and I were going on our honeymoon. I couldn't wait. I felt like my life was so very different from what it had been the last time I'd seen Jennifer. Just having her here really underlined for me the incredible path I'd found myself on, and yet looking back now, it seemed inevitable that I would end up here.

Jen was the best kind of guest. She was enthusiastic about everything and, as we drove out of Oxford, admired the scenery, the little villages we passed. As we headed towards Rafe's place, we seemed to find more and more things to talk about.

As we approached, she said, "So here's what I know about your guy. I know he's a respected antiquarian book special-ist"—she began ticking things off on her fingers—"and he still gives the odd lecture at Cardinal College. I know he's very good-looking, because I saw—not exactly a photograph of him on his website—but something that showed a very handsome man."

That was thanks to Theodore and Hester who, working together, had managed to custom-create something that was painted but very much looked like a photograph. It caught his serious, somewhat haughty expression. I loved that picture.

"Yes. That's him."

"Don't let me blunder into anything stupid. I really want him to like me."

"He will. And I really want you to like him, too. You guys are both so important to me." I didn't say I needed this to work, but on some level, I really felt like I did.

"And I know he's rich." She looked at me. "Anything I missed?"

A big one, but I couldn't bring myself to tell her. Not yet. "You've got the basics."

She looked at me. "I'm guessing, based on his experience and that photograph, he's what, mid-thirties?"

Give or take a few hundred years. I nodded.

"So five years older than you. That's not bad. Has he been married before?"

"Yes. Once. He was widowed."

"Widowed is good. Brokenhearted but not bitter?"

I smiled at her. "That's exactly how I would describe him. Brokenhearted but not bitter."

"Okay then. I think I'm ready."

I felt strangely nervous when we pulled up in front of the manor house. Henri, naturally, heard my car and came running like a hungry farmhand when the dinner gong goes. Jennifer was charmed by him, and I gave her one of the food pellets I kept in my car for the peacock. He stared at her for a minute with his beady eyes, took the pellet and then stood back and fanned out his tail. Poor Henri's tail was not as spectacular as some peacocks', but in the last little while, it had really plumped out. He was a rescue peacock who had flourished in his new environment. In some ways, Rafe was my rescue peacock. And under my care, I thought he was flourishing. Maybe that was arrogant, but I had seen the cold, distant vampire change into the loving creature he must have been when he was alive. He'd never be alive again, and I'd come to accept that, but we were going to make this work.

William must have been watching for us, because we hadn't even put our feet on the first step towards the front door when the double doors opened and he was standing there. He stepped forward with a smile beaming on his face.

"Lucy, you're right on time." He held out a hand and said, "And you must be Jennifer?"

She agreed that she was, and they shook hands. So far, so good. He asked her how she was enjoying Oxford and led us inside. William was a perfect combination of friendly and welcoming while never acting like he owned the place. I didn't know quite how he did it. It was a real art.

"Rafe is outside on the terrace. Lochlan Balfour is arriving any minute."

"From Ireland?"

His eyes lightened in a smile. "One never knows. He doesn't fly commercial."

Right. I was having trouble getting used to the idea of rubbing shoulders with billionaires. Somehow getting used to knitting with the undead had been easier.

"So he just drops out of the sky whenever he feels like it?"

"Basically, yes. He'll likely bring the helicopter. There's a spot on the property where he can land."

"Of course there is."

Actually, it made a lot of sense. No doubt Rafe had a helicopter too tucked away somewhere, something he hadn't yet told me about. I could imagine men like him and Lochlan Balfour were always ready to disappear at a moment's notice. Secrecy, money, and the ability to flee at the drop of a hat, all that would be part of my life now, too.

"Wow," I said. "You've got a full house."

He glanced at me. "Lucy, you know I like nothing more."

I was going to suggest that I give Jennifer a quick tour of the house, since her eyes had gone all wide and she was staring around her as though she'd stumbled into Buckingham Palace and no one had warned her, but then Rafe himself came in. He had on his most approachable expression, I was pleased to see. He shook Jennifer's hand and said how excited I'd been that she was coming. It was true.

She was still looking around in awe. "This place is fabulous. When Lucy told me about it, I don't know what I was expecting. But not this. This isn't a house. It's a castle!"

He smiled at her in that indulgent way he used to smile at me when I said things that he later told me made me sound like an American tourist.

He gave her a tour of the downstairs, and I made him show her the double walls of paintings that still tickled me. He had so many paintings that he had specially designed walls that opened out displaying a second level of artwork.

While Jen was marveling over a Monet, William came in. "I believe Lochlan's arriving."

Rafe excused himself and made his leisurely way out the doors that led to the back terrace. But obviously, we weren't going to stay inside while the excitement was happening. Jennifer and I hurried behind him. We were in time to see a black helicopter land on a grass field that was part of the landscaping, but had probably been kept like that precisely for helicopters to land on. No doubt Rafe came and went that way too, when it suited him.

Lochlan Balfour emerged from the helicopter. He wore dark jeans, a turtleneck T-shirt, and a blazer. He carried an attaché case. While we watched, a second man emerged and unloaded a suitcase. William hurried out to help. Lochlan, meanwhile, strode forward towards us, lifting one hand in a wave. The sun caught his hair, glinting gold.

Jennifer leaned closer and whispered, "I feel like I'm in a James Bond movie. You did not warn me you were surrounded by rich, powerful, gorgeous men. I might have to sit down."

I'd become so used to them, I'd almost forgotten what it was like at first. Wait till she saw them together. Dark and light and both incredibly good-looking. Introductions were soon made, and then we sat out on the stone veranda. It was beautifully shaded with wisteria but still felt open and airy, and we had the most beautiful view of the grounds. Olivia had outdone herself. I knew she'd been working night and day and had even hired some extra helpers to make sure the gardens and grounds were at their best for this very special day that was coming up. Naturally, talk quickly turned to the wedding. William, presumably having sorted out the luggage, came out and offered drinks.

"Champagne, I think," Rafe said, looking at me. He knew my weakness for champagne. I turned to Jennifer, who seemed to also think that was a spectacular idea. From the speed at which one of the vintage bottles of champagne that were kept in Rafe's cellar appeared, perfectly chilled and with four crystal wine flutes, I suspected that he and William had already talked this through. William popped the cork, poured the wine, and then Lochlan raised his glass. "If I may, I'd like to propose a toast to the happy couple. This is an Irish toast that seems appropriate.

"May joy and peace surround you

Contentment latch your door

And happiness be with you now

And bless you ever more."

He ended it by saying, "To Lucy and Rafe."

Jen echoed the toast, and then we all sipped our drinks.

"I hear you're from Boston," he said to Jen. "A lovely old city."

"It is, though not as old as Oxford."

I was really impressed with how cool Jennifer was, considering that sitting down with a tech mogul like Lochlan Balfour wasn't exactly an everyday experience. But we didn't talk about him or his businesses or computers. We talked about the wedding, mostly, then a little about current events.

We ended up staying outside for lunch and moving to an outdoor table. William served steak tartare to the vampires. The raw beef didn't look appetizing to me, but at least they could eat with us. William said to Jennifer, "I asked Lucy, and she thought you'd prefer something cooked. This salmon was flown down this morning from Scotland. It's served with a light dill sauce."

"Looks delicious," Jennifer said. And it was.

After lunch, Rafe said, "There's a very curious alchemy text I'd like to show you, Lochlan. Get your opinion on it."

Jennifer, who'd obviously grown very comfortable with the company and maybe even more outgoing than usual thanks to the champagne, said, "Ooh, is that part of your work? I'd love to see it."

Rafe paused only for an instant before saying in his usual suave manner, "Of course. Come along."

So the four of us trooped into his office, where he had all the most modern tools of his trade and any number of valuable volumes kept in a temperature-controlled case. He brought out the alchemy book that we'd found so puzzling.

Lochlan turned a couple of pages, looking as puzzled as I had. "But this is modern, surely?"

Obviously, Rafe didn't want to suggest that it had a spell on it since I hadn't had a chance to tell him yet that my old friend had also turned out to be a witch. He said, "What else do you notice about it?"

Lochlan turned a few more pages. "It's more obscure than most alchemical texts. Of course, I remember what Paracelsus used to say. Everything is poison, it just depends on the quantity."

Oh dear. Of course Lochlan could have known Paracelsus personally, back in the Middle Ages or whenever he was around practicing alchemy. But this really wasn't helping Jennifer's first impression of my fiancé and his best man.

As brightly as I could, I said, "Why don't we leave you two to it? I really want to show you the upstairs." Even I could hear the fake, brittle tone.

But Jennifer completely ignored me and stepped closer. She did a very strange thing. She took her hand and just hovered it above the pages, not touching it as I had done. Then she closed her eyes and leaned her whole body in.

"What are you—"

"Shh."

I shut up. The other two both glanced at me, and I shrugged my shoulders. I had no idea what she was doing.

Then she stepped back and, almost as though coming out of a trance, looked at me. "Lucy, could I see you outside for a minute?"

"Of course."

Oh, this first meeting was so not going the way I'd hoped it would.

I left two baffled vampires and took my best friend back into the corridor. "Sorry about that," I said. "They get a bit intense."

"Lucy. That book is spellbound."

"I know."

"What's going on?" She looked at me, and I had a hard time holding her gaze.

"What do you mean?"

"Who are those two? They're not witches, are they?"

"No, they're not."

She was looking at me, her faced creased in some emotion I couldn't name. Consternation? Horror? Plain curiosity?

"Lochlan Balfour talked about Paracelsus as though he'd known him. I remember studying him in chemistry. I barely remember it, but didn't he live in like the Middle Ages or something?"

I loved that her sense of history was about as good as mine. "I think so. He didn't exactly say that he knew him—"

"Don't toy with me, Lucy. We've known each other too long." She took in a deep breath. "I'm just going to ask. Are they vampires?"

She said it the way she might have asked if they were Republicans or Catholics. Not shocked, just curious. I nodded.

"Why didn't you tell me?"

"It's not exactly the easiest thing to share with anyone, even my best friend. I didn't know how you'd feel or how you'd react. I thought we'd meet today and you'd get to know him and then I'd sort of slip it into the conversation later."

She dragged me back to the terrace, and we sat back down. She glanced around to make sure we couldn't be overheard. "Lucy, are you sure about this?"

And I heaved a huge sigh. "See? That's why I didn't want to tell you. I knew you'd say this. You have to get to know Rafe to understand how amazing he is. And how happy he makes me."

"I could see that right away. You two are crazy about each other. It's just that you're going to get old."

"Do you think I don't know that? And he's not? I fought this for two years. But I don't want to fight it anymore. I love him. He loves me."

"Well, if he makes you happy, that's all that matters. And, realistically, he's the one with the most to lose." She settled back. "It's a lot to take in."

"Tell me about it."

"So how old are they?"

"Lochlan's older. I don't know exactly how old, but he was a Knight of the Garter, and I think that was in like the 1200s. I know that Rafe got turned into a vampire when Queen Elizabeth I was on the throne. He worked for her. He was a spy or something. That's how he got killed, and then saved by a vampire right before he died."

"Wow. I guess they've seen a lot." She laughed. "Weird to think of a vampire running a high-tech firm. It's so forward-thinking of him. Rafe's work makes a lot more sense. It's easier to imagine a vampire in dusty, book-lined corridors than in Silicon Valley."

"And yet they're great friends."

She settled back. "Okay. Are there any other big secrets you need to tell me? Because I'd rather get it all out in the open right now."

Oh my gosh, where to begin. "Well, Meri, an Egyptian grad student who you'll meet tomorrow, is really a two-thousand-year-old witch."

"Wait, what? Witches don't live two thousand years."

"This one did. She got cursed and trapped in a mirror, and I rescued her."

"I'll think about that later. What else?"

"Um, so my shop is home to a pretty special knitting club."

And then I told her all about the vampire knitting club. Her eyes grew round, and when I told her that they were my friends and that they were making my wedding dress, she burst out laughing.

"The older I get, the more I discover that the world is full of the most amazing things. So you're marrying a vampire, some of your best friends are vampires, and one of your guests is a two thousand-year-old witch. Okay."

"Oh, and one of the members of the vampire knitting club is also my grandmother."

"What?" She picked up her glass. "I am going to need some more champagne. Oh, and I'd really like to meet your grandmother."

And that made me so happy. Because I couldn't tell my own mother about Gran being alive. Mom was too strange about her magic. She'd rejected it her whole life, and now I suspected it was too late for her. She'd been nearly destroyed when a demon used her own magic against her, but Mom had somehow wiped the entire incident out of her mind. But to have Jennifer meet my grandmother—that was amazing. I'd told Gran so much about my best friend and my best friend so much about my grandmother. It just felt right.

Olivia appeared with a pair of pruning shears in her hand, and I called her over to meet Jen. "Olivia is William's sister. She keeps the grounds and is also doing our flowers for the wedding."

"That's amazing. It's going to be so beautiful. If you want any help, I love gardens and flowers. I'm a willing pair of hands, and I come free," Jen told her.

Olivia laughed. "What first-rate qualifications."

"You don't have to help with the wedding," I said when Olivia had left to get back to work.

"I want to. Besides, it will give me something useful to do when you're busy working."

CHAPTER 9

*T*he next day, Violet called in sick. She sounded so extravagantly sick, with a terrible cough and croaky voice, that I was sure she was faking.

I called Pete, since Meri didn't have a cell phone, and asked if she could help in the knitting shop. She agreed and sounded quite pleased at the prospect. Jennifer helped me open up. That didn't take long, so we stood there chatting until Meri arrived. With her was my mother.

She fussed over Jennifer and wanted to know about all the happenings at home. When customers began to arrive, I suggested they go next door and have coffee at Elderflower. They both seemed happy to go out for coffee. Mom said, loud enough that I could hear, "And Jennifer, you can help me plan the hen party."

I'd already regaled Jen with my horror over Mom's determination to have a hen party and my equal determination not to have one, so she sent me a laughing glance over my mother's shoulder.

"I'm counting on you," I said, hoping she could hear me.

Jen didn't come back, so I assumed she'd gone sightseeing.

Meri and I worked well together and were enjoying a successful day when Rafe came in later that afternoon looking grave. "Lucy, can I speak to you in private?"

Meri was comfortable enough that I had no problem leaving her alone for a while.

Once we were upstairs, Rafe said, "Where's Violet?"

"She called in 'sick.'" I put the word "sick" in air quotes. "I think she's having a poor Violet day. I'm not sure she wants to be single anymore, and it's hard to watch people you care about getting married. She's been so grumpy lately that it was almost a relief for her not to be here today."

He digested this. "Well, no reason for her to take her troubles out on you."

And that was an opinion I could totally get behind. "But you didn't come here to talk about Violet."

"No." He walked up and down, looked out the window as though the almost nonexistent traffic on Harrington Street fascinated him. "You're not going to like what I have to tell you," he said.

Before he could get further, Nyx came running down the stairs. She must have been sleeping on my bed upstairs and heard his voice. I thought I got pretty excited when Rafe turned up, but my passion was nothing compared with that of my cat. She was supposed to be my familiar, but she seemed to forget that whenever the handsome vampire was around. She meowed piteously, which I translated loosely to, "Love me, love me, love me."

He picked her up, and she immediately began to purr like

a chainsaw. She glanced at me with her green-gold eyes as though daring me to be jealous.

Rafe said, "You'd better sit down." And then he joined me, sitting by my side. Nyx immediately curled up on his lap, purring loudly. "I had the material in your rune box analyzed."

I didn't like the tone of his voice. "Okay."

"You have to understand, some of the top scientists in all the world practice here in Oxford. I don't think there can be any question."

I was really getting nervous now. "Spit it out, Rafe."

"If you had so much as tasted what was in that box, it would have killed you."

I hadn't been expecting good news, but getting death as a wedding present? I hadn't seen that one coming.

I asked the obvious question. "Are you sure?"

"Believe me, I had them test it a second time. The ingredients are altogether curious. But it's the arsenic that would have killed you."

I was stunned. "Who would do such a thing? Who hates me that much?"

He took my hand. "That's a question that's puzzling me, too. Think, Lucy. Have you upset someone?"

"No. Not that I can think of."

I looked down at Nyx, who was so possessive about Rafe, and wondered if someone had tried to get rid of me in hopes of winning my fiancé when I was gone. "What about you? Could there be someone so infatuated with you that they would get rid of me rather than see you married and unavailable?"

He looked at me the way my mother used to when she caught me reading a Harlequin romance. "Really, Lucy."

"What? It's possible."

And then he just said, "No."

Which was rather comforting.

I said, "I think I know where this came from. Rafe, this is witch business. Do you have proof that the stuff in that box was laced with arsenic?"

He nodded and withdrew a piece of paper from his inner pocket. "This is the breakdown of ingredients that were identified. A couple of them puzzled even the top chemists. They're still trying to identify them. But I only care about the poison."

I nodded. We both knew there were substances that mere mortals knew nothing about. But I didn't like that somebody had tried to kill me with an old standby like arsenic.

The downstairs door opened and closed, and I heard footsteps on the stairs. There were very few people who would come up to my flat unannounced, so I suspected immediately it was my grandmother. Sure enough, Gran came into the room. But instead of looking like my comfortable Gran, she looked shaken and pale, even for her.

"Oh, Lucy, the most terrible thing happened," my grandmother said.

Sylvia followed her, looking grim and somehow guilty. "Oh, Rafe. You're here." She sounded as though she wished he weren't.

"What happened?" I asked them.

They came all the way into the lounge, and Gran said, "I'm sorry, dear. I didn't know Rafe was here."

He said, "Would you like me to leave?"

"No," I answered before they could. I had a sneaking suspicion I might need him, depending on why these two were looking guilty and upset. "That's okay. What's going on?"

Gran squeezed her hands together. "I couldn't sleep, you see. It's the excitement over the wedding. And there's so much to do. I just popped out to get some seed pear—" She glanced at Rafe. "Some things, and I bumped smack into Mrs. Darlington."

Now I saw why she was looking so horrified. "Mrs. Darlington, our customer?"

"That's the one. She's got the daughter your age and three boys. Knits a lot of sweaters."

I nodded. "What exactly happened?"

This was disastrous, but I wasn't sure yet how disastrous. Based on the expressions on these two vampires' faces, though, it was on the bad end of disastrous.

"I smacked right into her. I was thinking about something else or I never would have gone out at all. Not in the middle of the day." And with my mother and father in town, she'd promised me she'd stay out of sight. But yelling at her wasn't going to help. I kept my voice calm.

"You bumped into her, and then what happened?"

"Well, she looked so pleased to see me. She said, 'Agnes Bartlett.' And I, of course, complimented her on the sweater she was wearing. It was really very lovely. One of the Teddy Lamont designs, done in shades of mauve."

"Never mind her sweater," I said with what patience I could muster. I was picturing this as though the scene were happening in front of me, and I couldn't even imagine where it was going from here.

"I was about to ask after her husband when it suddenly it struck me that I probably shouldn't be talking to her at all."

Really?

"I made to walk away, and then Mrs. Darlington grabbed her chest, took a step back and said, 'Wait a minute. I thought you died.'"

Oh dear, oh dear.

"That's when I told Agnes to do the forgetting spell," Sylvia put in.

"But there were so many people around, I didn't dare."

"So, what did you do?" If Mrs. Darlington was running around claiming she'd seen my dead grandmother, then we were going to have all kinds of problems.

"Sylvia dragged her off the High Street and into an alley."

I didn't think the story could get worse. And then it did. "You did what?"

"It was all I could think of," Sylvia said, sounding defensive.

Mrs. Darlington had brought up three rough-and-tumble boys. I doubted very much that she'd gone willingly into a back alley with two old ladies.

"Who knew she had such lungs on her?" Sylvia said, confirming what I'd feared.

"So you dragged a screaming woman down into an alley?" I glanced at Rafe, but he sat still as stone. And as impassive. He'd probably been witness to worse disasters, but I hadn't.

"It was all we could think of. We had to get her away from the crowd so that Agnes could do her forgetting spell."

"Did anyone follow you?" Rafe asked. Excellent question.

"Two large men. They said, 'Hey there, what you doing?'"

Sylvia, being an actress, managed to sound like a local man with a deep voice.

Oh, this was not good.

"Were the police involved?" Another excellent question. I was so glad I'd told Rafe to remain.

"No. It didn't come to that. I have to say, Sylvia showed great presence of mind," Gran said admiringly. "I was in a panic. One woman screaming and struggling, two burly men bearing down on me as though I were a common criminal. I went quite blank with fright."

I was feeling quite blank with fright myself.

Gran continued, "But Sylvia was as calm as a cucumber. While the men were advancing on me, she opened the door that leads down a steep flight of stairs into the tunnels. She pushed the men through the door."

I stared at Sylvia, who said rather smugly, "We're much stronger than we look."

"Then I managed the forgetting spell on poor Mrs. Darlington. I had to hide myself the minute I did it, and then Sylvia helped her back out to the street, where she wandered off looking slightly confused but with no memory of me."

"And what happened to the two men you pushed down the stairs?" I asked Sylvia.

"Here we come to the problem. I'm afraid I had to tie them up and gag them. In order for your grandmother to do her forgetting spell, they need to be somewhere where it's logical for them to be. Not tied up in a dark tunnel underneath the streets of Oxford."

Only one part of that sentence had lodged into my brain like a huge thorn. "They're still down there?"

"They are. We're in a bit of a quandary. Don't know what to do with them."

I glanced at Rafe, who still looked carefully expressionless, though there was some tension around his jaw that suggested he might be clenching his teeth.

He thought about it for a moment. We all remained quiet as he made a decision. I felt sweat begin to pool everywhere sweat could. I had a mental image of two huge and angry men breaking out of their bonds and causing havoc. "Right. Get Theodore and Alfred up, and they can keep a watch. I'm sorry for it, but they'll have to stay there until after dark, when we can move them."

"I'll get Theodore and Alfred," Sylvia said, when Gran rose. "You stay here."

Gran slumped on the couch as though her legs wouldn't hold her anymore. "I feel terrible. I'm so sorry to cause you this trouble."

I sat beside her and patted her hand. "I know you didn't mean it, but this can't go on, Gran."

She nodded at me, looking sad. "I know, dear. I've so loved being here to help you get the shop running and on its feet, but you have Rafe now. You'll be a married woman soon." She looked at him appealingly. "I know I'll have to leave Oxford, but would you mind very much if I stay until after the wedding? I'd so like to see my granddaughter get married. And then I'll go somewhere far away." She sounded so sad, I felt tears prick at my eyes. I didn't want to lose her.

"Of course," Rafe answered. At least I'd have Gran nearby a little longer.

"While you're here, can you think of any reason why Karmen, the witch in Wallingford, might want to kill me?"

Gran had obviously been worrying about the men downstairs, but now she sharpened her gaze on mine. "Kill you? Why would she do that?"

"I was wondering if you might know."

She looked stunned. "Are you certain?"

I went through the gift arriving at Rafe's place and how he'd had the contents of the box analyzed and found it contained massive amounts of arsenic.

"I wonder if Sylvia might know something," she said.

"Know something about what?" Sylvia asked, returning from her errand. I sometimes forgot how fast vampires could move when they wanted to.

"Everything all right?" Rafe asked her.

"Yes. Alfred and Theodore are both keeping watch. Don't worry. We'll take those men somewhere safe tonight, put lots of alcohol around them, and Agnes will do her forgetting spell. They'll think they got intoxicated at the pub."

"Good."

Gran looked at her old friend. "We've been talking of me leaving Oxford. I'm afraid it's time."

Sylvia looked sad too. She said, "Wherever you go, Agnes, I shall go with you. You'd be lost without me. Besides, I was the one who turned you into a vampire. I feel you're my responsibility."

My grandmother perked up a bit. "I'd be glad of the company, but where shall we go?"

Sylvia shrugged fatalistically. "Wherever you like, my dear. New York, Seattle, Toronto, Reykjavik."

"But these are all so far away," I cried. "I want you to be close enough that I can visit you, Gran."

Rafe said, "Cornwall."

We all turned to stare at him. "Cornwall?" I don't know why; it just seemed like such an odd choice of locations.

He nodded. "I own a manor house there. A couple rented it from me for the last twenty years or so and ran it as a B&B. But they're getting on and wish to retire, so they've told me they plan to end their lease. There's an old tin mine on the property." He didn't say more, but I thought a tin mine was underground, just like the lair they'd built here in the tunnels under Oxford. I bet they could make a tin mine very comfortable. Unless they just wanted to live in the manor house.

"Cornwall," Gran said, perking up. "I spent my honeymoon there. Though no one would remember me, of course. I don't think I was ever back again. It was lovely though. Very rugged coast, fascinating history. And they have their own style of knitting that's quite remarkable." I could see her getting quite enthusiastic about this idea.

Sylvia seemed less enthusiastic at first but soon came around to the idea when she realized that they could simply drive down there in the Bentley. Rafe said, "Why don't you go and check it out now and come back in time for the wedding?"

I thought that was a really good idea. Just in case Gran's forgetting spell hadn't worked as well on Mrs. Darlington as we might have hoped, she wouldn't be here if the woman came looking for her. If anyone came looking for her. Gran's magic wasn't as strong as it had been when she was alive. In fact, I decided I'd better go along tonight and perform the forgetting spells.

"But I don't want to leave you. There's so much preparation still to be done for your wedding."

I gripped her hand. "And I don't want you to go, but Mom's here. She wants to help with the preparations too."

"Well, it makes me very sad, but it's more her right than mine to help her daughter prepare for her wedding day."

"But you'll still come back for the big day. I'm sorry we'll have to hide you away, but you'll have an excellent view from the window. We'll make sure of it."

"My dear, I couldn't ask for anything more. The vampires will know where I am. They'll come and visit. I won't be lonely."

"That's settled then." And what a great relief it was. I really hoped that Gran and Sylvia fell in love with Cornwall. It seemed like the perfect solution: far enough away that no one would recognize them but close enough that we could still see each other.

"Right," Sylvia said, rising. "I think we could both use a bit of a nap after all that excitement."

Gran rose to follow her and then saw the paper with all the chemical squiggles on my coffee table. She looked at it curiously, then at me. "What's that, dear?"

"Oh, right. That's the chemical analysis of the contents of the mysterious box that promised the elixir of youth, but in fact, it contained poison."

"What!" Sylvia shrieked. I jumped at the sound. She hadn't sounded that furious since I'd lost her priceless necklace.

I turned to her. "Do you know something about this?" I'd had my suspicions.

She looked rather sheepish. "It was me who gave it to you. And it was a very expensive gift."

Sometimes, the workings of Sylvia's mind were a complete mystery. "Why didn't you sign the note?"

"I did. I signed it, 'An admirer.' And I am a great admirer of yours. I don't always tell you how much I appreciate you, but—"

"Never mind that. Did you get the box from Karmen in Wallingford?"

"Where else? It was obvious she'd made a success of her alchemy. If you don't want to be turned into a vampire, this is a perfect alternative. You'll still be human, you'll still be a witch, but you'll stay young and beautiful forever. And Rafe won't lose another wife."

I was touched by her generosity, but also horrified. "So you had no idea what was in this box?"

"Of course not. She assured me that only she knew the recipe and made me swear you wouldn't tell anyone about the elixir or try to sell it."

"But why would she poison it?" I asked the room. "It makes no sense. I haven't done anything to her. Okay, I called her on selling hexes, but it's not like we ended up sworn enemies." I didn't like the sound of this at all. "I'm going over there." I didn't relish a second confrontation with this witch, but I thought I deserved some straight answers.

"I'm coming with you," said Rafe.

"Well, I will not be left behind," said Sylvia. "I deserve some answers, too. And a refund."

"I suppose I'll have to stay here," Gran said, "as Karmen knows me." And then she turned to me. "But I think you should take Margaret Twigg. Margaret may be the only witch who can keep this one in line."

I wanted to take Margaret Twigg along about as much as I

wanted to face down a witch who'd pretty much tried to murder me, but Gran was right. Rafe and Sylvia were strong and powerful, but they weren't our kind.

However, when I called Margaret Twigg, she didn't pick up.

We'd go without her.

CHAPTER 10

I hadn't warmed to Karmen, the Wicked Witch of Wallingford, and I'd definitely been wary of a woman who'd sell hexes that caused the amount of damage poor Violet had sustained, but I hadn't thought she would try to murder me. I still didn't understand why she would. She had to know there were going to be consequences.

And the consequences were on their way.

I was glad that Rafe and I were driving separately from Sylvia, because it was really important we got there first. Sylvia in the Bentley would, with any luck, arrive after me and Rafe in the Tesla.

I found my hands were trembling with the combination of rage and trepidation. I didn't enjoy having enemies. Yet, somehow, I'd managed to get myself a deadly one. Margaret Twigg had been warning me that dark forces were coming. Was this what she'd meant?

I'd imagined a big confrontation between good witches and bad witches, not that I would be the victim of a single, mean witch. What had I ever done to Karmen? When I voiced this idea, Rafe looked at me.

"Maybe she's jealous."

"Jealous of me?" It was ludicrous.

He shrugged. "A woman who will work that hard to look eternally young and beautiful might be overcome with rage seeing your actual youth and beauty. She could never quite recapture a bloom like yours."

Okay, I bathed in the compliment for a bit, the way I'd roll around in a scented, warm bubble bath. Then I took in what he was really saying. "But if she had killed me, she had to know that Sylvia would come after her."

"She may not know exactly what Sylvia is capable of. In fact, she may not know that Sylvia is undead."

It was true enough. We hadn't exactly advertised the fact, and we'd done the tea mug switching thing. Still, there was something about Sylvia that screamed, "Do not cross me."

But maybe the Wicked Witch of Wallingford was so confident of her own powers that she believed she could take Sylvia. Maybe she'd assumed Sylvia would taste the elixir, not knowing that Sylvia didn't need it.

One way or another, it was showdown time.

As we grew nearer, I spotted a car coming towards us in the other lane. I didn't know why I looked at it. I'm not one of those people who loves cars so much they like to pick out makes and models as they drive by. It was an inborn instinct. That power that people kept telling me I had and that I was working to try and control.

The car drove by, and as I looked into it, I saw Margaret Twigg. Her face looked peculiar. Set and hard and angry.

Well, that part wasn't peculiar, except that normally she only looked like that when she was looking at me.

"That's Margaret Twigg," I said aloud.

"Not that surprising. This is the main road back to Oxford."

"Huh, I wonder what she was doing out here."

I directed Rafe to Karmen's house, and as we pulled up, he looked around. "I remember this pub. I used to frequent it back when Sylvia was still making films."

It was always weird when he gave me glimpses of his past, something he was doing more and more now that we were committed to each other.

I said, "It belongs to a witch now."

He nodded. "It did then, too. But the beer was excellent."

The lights were on in the old pub but not in the house. I said, "Let's take a trip down memory lane. You can see what the old place looks like now. No doubt Karmen is mixing up more of her magic potion for skin creams."

He said, "Question her carefully. Remember, we want to know why she tried to kill you."

Now that we were here, I didn't even want to go inside. I felt like a coward. All I wanted to do was get rid of that poison and forget the whole incident had ever happened. But I knew I couldn't do that. I had to stop this woman from trying to kill other witches. It was bad enough when she'd made both Violet and Felicity Stevens so sick, but what was in that box would have killed me. Not cool.

Rafe obviously sensed my hesitation. "Do you want me to go in alone?" His voice sounded calm, but I saw the way his fingers tightened. I worried that his love for me might make him more revengeful and less cool than he thought he could remain. That made me brave enough to get out of the car.

"Let's do this thing. We have to make a pact. Just because she tried to hurt me doesn't mean that we hurt her. Two wrongs don't make a right."

"You may need to remind me of that again. The thought of her hurting you makes my blood boil." He turned to stare at me. "And I'm relatively cold-blooded."

I took his hand, and we walked forward. I knocked on the door, but there was no answer. I could see Rafe was about to break it open, but I stopped him.

"I have an unlocking spell." I was always so pleased when I had spells at the ready that I had memorized and knew worked.

I closed my eyes, whispered the words that would unlock the door and heard the quiet click of the lock. I turned the handle and opened the door. The lights were on, and Tilda was working away over a couple of steaming pots on the big gas stove. I smelled those familiar scents, the licorice, the lavender and rose, and that musky something else that I still hadn't put my finger on. Soft harp music was playing. But of Karmen there was no sign.

We both walked in, and then I said, loud enough that she could hear me but hopefully not loud enough that I scared the woman to death, "Tilda?"

She started and turned to look at me. Her face was slightly flushed from the steam, and tendrils of her gray hair were curling around her face. Once again, I thought how very different this naturally aging older woman looked from her glamorous employer. She blinked at me. "I'm sorry. I've forgotten your name."

"It's Lucy. And this is my fiancé Rafe. We're looking for Karmen."

She blinked at me as though not sure what to say. "Karmen doesn't see customers unless you have an appointment."

"I'm not here to buy anything," I said, cool and steely. Or as close to cool and steely as I could get. "Do you know where she is?"

"No. She was at home earlier, but she may have gone out again. I don't keep track."

"Thanks."

We closed the door and went back outside. The Bentley pulled up behind the Tesla, and Sylvia got out. Alfred was once again her driver, and I had a feeling that he'd also come along to make sure she didn't tear anybody's throat out.

"Aren't you supposed to be guarding those men?" I asked him.

"Christopher Weaver took my place. Thought you might need me."

"Where is she?" Sylvia asked in a voice that made my blood run cold.

"She's not in there," I said.

"She must be in the house then."

"But there are no lights on in the cottage. Her assistant, Tilda, said she might be out somewhere."

Then Sylvia threw back her head and sniffed like a bloodhound. It was easy to forget that behind the elegant façade was a creature extremely good at scenting blood. Rafe and Alfred hadn't been around Karmen, but Sylvia had.

Alfred set his long nose to quivering and then said,

"There's an *O* blood type in the pub over there." He wrinkled his nose. "So common."

He was a connoisseur of blood types.

Sylvia shook her head. "That's not her. That's the assistant."

She stepped closer to the house and drew in a deep breath. "She's inside."

I wondered why Karmen had the lights off. The day was cloudy, and her cottage hadn't been big on windows anyway. Maybe she'd seen us coming and plunged the house into darkness, hoping we'd go away. That's what I'd do if Sylvia was after me on the warpath.

I made to do my unlocking trick again, but Sylvia pushed the front door and it opened wide. It wasn't locked.

Sylvia might be good at smelling out blood, but I sensed energy. I'd felt that hint of cold darkness in the air when we'd come before. This time I felt something darker and muddier.

"Karmen?" I called.

We all walked in. "Split up," Rafe said. I nodded. He said, "Lucy with me. Alfred and Sylvia together."

I'd thought he'd meant to split up into singles, but then I realized he didn't want Sylvia coming across that witch by herself. He wanted Alfred with her, and even more, he wanted us to find the witch first.

Okay, I couldn't lock onto someone based on the blood pumping through their veins, but I had my witch intuition. In the same way I'd been able to sense Margaret Twigg on a highway, I should be able to find Karmen in her own house. I closed my eyes for a second and then headed towards the living room.

And found her there.

She lay on the rug, one arm stretched out. The evening was growing dim, so I switched on a light and then cried out in horror.

"That's not Karmen," I said. There was an old woman lying there. Wrinkled and hag-like. Her legs and arms were spindly, the gray flesh sagging from them, her hair gray and thin and matted. And then I noticed the pointed finger. It was twisted and knobby with arthritis, but the fingernail was oval and painted pale pink. I ran forward. Dropped to my knees beside her. "Karmen?"

She wasn't dead, but it was close. I could feel her life force seeping away and the darkness of death pressing down on her.

I touched her shoulder. Her eyes flickered open, and she gave a great gasping breath. She looked past me to Rafe. "The book," she said.

"Book? What book? Karmen, what happened?" I asked her.

But there was no answer. Karmen's life force was faint, and I saw the moment it ended.

"She's dead," I said, as though that weren't obvious.

Rafe nodded.

"Gran was right. This must be the same Karmen she'd known. She was young and beautiful a few days ago, but when she was dying, the elixir must have stopped working." She definitely looked her age.

Her last words had been, "the book." I looked around. There was a small bookcase in a corner. "What book do you think she was talking about?"

He shook his head. "No idea."

Sylvia and Alfred walked in then. Sylvia looked down at the dead witch and said, "Is that old crone Karmen?"

I nodded. Sylvia sniffed the air. "Her blood wasn't spilled."

Rafe answered her. "No. I'm not sure how she died. Blunt force trauma or poison, I'd guess."

I didn't want to hazard a guess, but Karmen could have died of old age.

"You believe she was murdered?" Sylvia asked.

"Seems most likely," Rafe said.

"I suggest we get out of here before the authorities arrive," Sylvia said.

Before we left, I perused the bookshelf, but the titles were so safe they could have been props. There were coffee-table books on gardening and history. The kind of novels that book clubs tended to read or judging panels gave awards to. I was not seeing anything here that would cause a witch to be killed. There were no books on witchcraft, nothing but bland titles suitable for a public library, and there were no missing spots where a missing book had been.

I turned around. Karmen hadn't been very nice and had presumably sent me a box containing poison, but still I didn't want to just leave her here. I said to Rafe, "We should call the police."

Sylvia made a rude noise. "Well, I won't be here. Anyway, it's quite obvious. Her employee must have done it. She's the only other one here."

I turned to stare at her. "Why would Tilda murder her boss? She just did herself out of a job. Anyway, if she was behind this, would she really have stayed behind in the pub making cold cream?"

Sylvia shrugged her elegant shoulders. "Daywalkers never cease to surprise me with their stupidity." Then she crooked a finger at Alfred. "Come along. These two can do whatever they like, but I suggest you and I get on the road back to Oxford."

Alfred seemed perfectly happy to comply, only pausing long enough to say, "Will you two be all right?"

"We will," Rafe said.

After Alfred and Sylvia left, Rafe stood and took a quick look around the living room. He said, "I rarely agree with Sylvia, but she might be right, you know. Perhaps we should leave."

I shook my head. "Even if we wanted to, Tilda knows we were here." The last thing I needed was to get involved with the police again. It was one thing to report a crime, quite another to have the police chase you up because you'd been on the scene where a murder was committed and then left. However, I knew that Rafe liked to keep a low profile in Oxfordshire for obvious reasons. I said, "Why don't you go. I can call it in." Listen to me, sounding like a bad cop show.

He looked at me as though he were disappointed. "You know I'm not going to leave you." Of course I did.

"I'm sorry," I said. I was, too. I hated dragging him into danger or even just awkward social situations. Between the wedding and me being a witch and not a vampire, I seemed to be forever dragging him into a limelight he would have preferred to avoid.

Still, he didn't have to marry me, did he? It was his idea.

I rubbed my thumb along the top of my engagement ring, as I tended to do when I needed reassurance. Or a reminder that we were really getting married. "I'll call them now."

I made the call and agreed that I would stay where I was until the authorities arrived.

"There's no point standing here with a dead witch. I'd better go and tell poor Tilda."

He looked at me with a frown between his eyes. "Sylvia isn't always tactful, but she might be right. Be very careful around Tilda. And you're not going to talk to her alone."

I shook my head. I stuck to my opinion that a woman who'd killed her boss would hardly hang around, still working. Still, I knew he was right and I should be careful.

It was a relief to go back outside and leave the heavy darkness, not only of death but of the negative witch energy that Karmen had put out. My shoes crunched across the gravel as I headed to the former pub. Rafe shut the door softly and was only a step behind me.

I walked in and found the scene very much as it had been when we arrived. Tilda was still at work at a pot on the stove. Harp music still played. It was very peaceful and smelled of herbs and flowers. I hated to intrude on her with such terrible news, but I thought it was better coming from me than the police. Between the music and the bubbling mixture, she didn't hear the door, so I called out, "Tilda?"

She jumped a little bit, as I'd obviously surprised her, and then she turned around. "Oh, it's you, Lucy. I forgot to lock the door. Did you find Karmen?" She looked at me, all innocent. Oh, I hated to be the one to tell her.

I said, "Why don't you come out of the kitchen for a minute and sit down. I need to talk to you."

She glanced at her mixture and then turned off the burner. Good plan.

She wiped her hands on her apron and came out looking puzzled. "What's the matter?"

I said, "Please, sit down." I sat down too at the scarred table that they used for packaging things.

"Tilda, I'm sorry to be the one to tell you this, but Karmen's dead."

CHAPTER 11

*H*er eyes opened slowly wider and wider, and then she blinked once. "Karmen's dead?" she asked as though she couldn't believe it.

I reached for her hand. It was warm and slightly damp from where she'd been stirring the mixture. "I am so sorry. I found her in her house. She'd collapsed."

Tilda put her other hand to her heart as though to check that she was still alive. "But I just saw her earlier. She seemed —" And then her face creased in a worried frown. "She was complaining of a headache and chest pains. I thought she'd been overdoing it. That's why she left me here to finish up this batch."

And yet she hadn't said that to us when we'd arrived. She'd only said that she didn't know where her boss was.

"How long had she been complaining of headaches and chest pain?" I asked. I'd been involved in enough suspicious deaths that it had become second nature to me to ask probing questions. Not that the police ever appreciated my inter-ference.

Tilda looked as though she was having trouble taking in what I was saying. "I can't believe it. You're certain? She doesn't need a doctor?"

I shook my head again. "She's beyond a doctor. I'm so sorry. I've called the police. They'll be here soon."

Beneath my hands, hers jerked. "Police. Oh dear, oh dear. Poor Karmen."

No doubt they'd be asking Tilda to identify her boss, so I felt I should at least prepare her for what she might be about to see. "She looks very old."

She looked confused again. "Who does?"

"Karmen. She doesn't look the same as she did. She looks like a very old woman."

"But that's ridiculous. She can't be more than forty-five at the most."

"I'm just telling you what I saw. I don't want you to be shocked."

She scrunched up her face as though faced with a difficult math problem. Gently, I said, "You must have known she was a witch."

Now she pulled her hand away from mine. "It's not nice to speak ill of the dead."

Hey, I was a witch. Since when was that an insult? I merely said, "I have every respect for the craft. But I think she may have been older than she looked."

She waved a hand around the shelves filled with the distinctive dark blue bottles. "It was her cosmetics. The cream is wonderful. That's all."

Again, I didn't want to be insulting, but I said, "Do you use the creams?"

"Of course, I do. I get an excellent discount. I use them faithfully, day and night."

"And yet you don't look forty." Sixty, at a guess.

She looked at me as though I'd hit her. I was not doing well in the winning friends and influencing people department. "I do the best I can. I admit, Karmen cared more about her appearance than I did. I'm sure she wasn't above helping nature along, if you know what I mean."

I didn't entirely. "Are you suggesting she used surgery and facelifts and so on to stay young? Or do you mean she used witchcraft?"

She let out a huge sigh. "I never inquired too deeply. She stayed remarkably young looking. And, of course, it helped the business enormously. I always got a nice bonus every year." She looked around again, now forlorn. "I suppose that's all over."

I thought, not only was that woman not going to get any more bonuses, but she was most likely out of a job.

"Do you know anything about Karmen's family?"

She shook her head. "She didn't have any. Friends, of course, and everyone in Wallingford knew her."

"I wonder what will happen to her estate?"

Tilda suddenly pulled herself together and looked offended. "That's hardly your business."

I could see she was overcoming her shock and probably becoming protective of the woman who had employed her.

"I'm sorry. You're right. Her death has thrown me, too."

She stood up and said, "Why don't you head on home now. I can take care of the police. I should make sure she's comfortable." And then her face crumpled and she began to cry.

Obviously, Rafe and I couldn't let her go into the house. If it was a murder scene, the last thing the police would want was more people blundering around in there, obscuring any clues.

However, Tilda wasn't thinking straight, and I'd promised the police I wouldn't leave the scene.

Luckily, my sharp ears picked up the sound of approaching cars. Sure enough, two police cars pulled into the drive. I stepped out of the pub to greet them. There were two uniforms from Thames Valley Police, and in the second car was the coroner.

We waited outside while they went in and had a brief look around, and then a woman who introduced herself as PC Dunford came out to take my statement and Rafe's. Obviously, I didn't tell her my reason for visiting Karmen was that she had sold one of my wedding guests a poisoned version of the elixir of life. I said, instead, that I had purchased some face cream and bridesmaid gifts from her, which was true and easily checkable, and had come back to talk to her about her products because I'd liked them so much. That seemed plausible.

More vehicles began to arrive. Tilda came out of the pub and looked around as though she'd stepped into a nightmare. After giving our names and contact information, we were allowed to leave.

On the drive back to Oxford, Rafe said, "That was very unfortunate."

"That's an understatement."

"I don't like this, Lucy. I don't like it at all. That woman sent you poisoned elixir of life and then was herself poisoned."

I didn't like where his thoughts were heading either. "We don't know that she was poisoned. You saw how old she was. Couldn't she have died of natural causes?"

"No."

"Okay, she could have been bashed over the head or, I don't know, smothered or something." She hadn't been strangled, because there weren't any marks on her neck. Or were there? She was so shriveled and her skin so old that there were odd marks and blemishes consistent with aging.

"We'll wait until the postmortem's been done, but I want you to be very careful."

"Why?" It would help if he would articulate what he was hinting at.

"If you were sent poison, and she was poisoned, it's possible that the killer will try again to finish you off."

"But why would anyone want to kill both me and Karmen? There was no connection between us."

He sent me a disbelieving look. "I can think of one obvious connection."

"Well, okay, we're both witches. But so is Margaret Twigg a witch and—" Just mentioning her name made me recall that I had seen her driving away from Wallingford as we'd been driving towards it. I turned to him. "Rafe. Margaret Twigg was heading back to Oxford when we were on our way to see Karmen. Remember?"

He kept his eyes on the road but nodded. "Are you suggesting that Margaret Twigg might have killed a rival witch?"

"Not really. It does seem kind of a stretch. But it's an odd coincidence, don't you think?"

"Lucy, this is a reasonably well-traveled road. There could

be any number of reasons why Margaret Twigg would be on it, and she was certainly headed back in the direction of her cottage."

That was true. I was probably looking for trouble where none existed. "Still, if you were looking for a connection between me and Karmen, Margaret Twigg would be one. I don't think she was very pleased that the Wicked Witch of Wallingford sold a hex to someone in Oxford or that the hex was intended for a fellow witch."

He nodded slowly. "You think she might have confronted Karmen? That is interesting."

And then I sucked in breath so hard I choked on my own tongue and started to cough. He looked at me sideways. "Are you all right?"

I shook my head. My throat was kind of burning, and my eyes were stinging. It took me a second to command my voice. "Violet."

He turned to me. "Violet?"

"It was Violet who suffered from the hex." I smacked myself on the forehead. "And I told her about it. She was so snarky and in such a bad mood when I took the afternoon off to go to Wallingford. And the next day we were in the shop together and I was subjected to all these miserable comments about how nice it was for me to have the afternoon off while she'd been stuck in the shop working."

"She does get paid for her hours in your shop, doesn't she?"

"Tell me about it. But she doesn't see it that way."

"I understand Violet is your cousin, but she's never going to make employee of the month, is she?"

He could say that again.

"And today she didn't come to work." I could hear again the fake coughing and wheezing on the phone this morning. "What if she took the day off in order to come down here and confront Karmen? What if she killed her?"

"Let's not jump to conclusions. She is your cousin. Are you certain she wasn't genuinely ill?"

I shook my head. "She called this morning and made a big production of coughing and sniffling. Said she had a terrible headache and didn't feel well and that she'd be spending the day in bed."

"And you disbelieve her?"

"She was fine yesterday. And then suddenly today, she's so ill she can't come into work? She was faking it. But I just assumed she was still mad at me because I had taken an afternoon off without her and she was going to pay me back."

"That does sound rather like something Violet would do."

Still, I was really stretching here. "But would she really go and kill the woman who'd put the hex on her? I mean, Karmen didn't even put the hex on her. She just sold the hex to someone who put it on Violet."

"It was a very violent hex, though." Rafe seemed to be thinking. I was thinking, too, and furiously.

I shook my head. "I can't believe Violet would kill another witch."

"Perhaps she didn't plan to."

I leaned back, closing my eyes and resting my head against the seatback. "I can't believe two of the witches I'm closest to I'm now suspecting of murdering yet another of our sisters."

"One could definitely argue that the world of witches will be better without Karmen."

"Still, we don't take vigilante justice into our own hands like that. First, do no harm."

"I do not believe that Karmen lived by that rule."

That was for sure. And Margaret Twigg would be the first one to want to punish a witch who brought bad magic to Margaret's own territory.

And then Violet had very personal reasons to want revenge on Karmen.

CHAPTER 12

I replayed the scene in my mind when we'd found the witch Karmen. Not quite dead. And with her last bit of energy, she'd said, "The book." I opened my eyes again and turned to Rafe. "What about her last words? She said, 'The book,' and then she died."

"I've been wondering that, too. What could it mean?"

"I don't know. But she was looking right at you when she said it."

"I'm not sure in her final moments she really focused on anything."

I wasn't so sure about that. "What did your friend the don say about that book you wanted to discuss with him?"

He turned to me in surprise, as though I was changing the subject, but I wasn't sure I was. "You mean that strange alchemy book?"

"Yes."

"It's a hobby of his, studying alchemy. It helps pass the time."

"Is he a vampire?"

"Yes. He is."

"How come I don't know him?"

He looked slightly amused. "We don't all knit. Some of us collect stamps or renovate houses. He studies alchemy."

"Did he have any ideas about the book?"

"Why are you asking this?"

"Because she looked at you and said, 'The book,' and I'm wondering if she could have been referring to that book."

He paused before answering. "Because we suspect her of being an alchemist, and that was an alchemy book?"

"A spellbound alchemy book. She's both a witch and an alchemist." Okay, it was a bit of a stretch, but it was kind of weird that the alchemy book had turned up right around the same time that she was selling hexes to hurt Violet. Now it turned out Karmen had been an alchemist. But then, Rafe got sent all kinds of strange books. Maybe there was no connection. Still, my intuition was tingling.

"Have you had any other strange and peculiar books come into your life recently?"

He took the turn-off into Oxford. "A very nice first edition of *Lorna Doone*. And your father was telling me about some scrolls he'd like me to go and have a look at."

I'd call that a no.

Naturally, my grim work wasn't done for the day. There were still two men in the tunnels to be magicked into forgetting they'd seen two old ladies attack a middle-aged one and then been confined in a dark tunnel for several hours.

Gran said she could do the forgetting spell, but I knew my magic was stronger.

That made me think about Gran moving away. "Are you sure Gran will be happy in Cornwall?"

"I can't make anyone happy. All I can do is offer her a place to live where she'll be safe."

"Will she be bored, though?"

"Not if she's kept busy." He pulled up in front of Cardinal Woolsey's. "What do you think about buying her a shop to run?"

I glanced at the pretty shop Gran had passed on to me. "You mean franchise Cardinal Woolsey's?" Look at me, the successful entrepreneur.

"Exactly. We've talked about it before. You'd have economies of scale, and your grandmother would have a knitting shop again. It would keep her busy, and you could go and visit her whenever you wanted to. It's only about a five-hour drive to Cornwall in good conditions."

I was excited by the idea. "I think it's brilliant. Now all we have to do is wipe the memories of the men who could cause us all a heap of trouble."

"We?" He raised his eyebrows in my direction.

"You didn't really think I was going to leave my grandmother to do the forgetting spell, did you? I'm coming with you."

He was smart enough not to waste time arguing.

"You were late home last night," Jen said when I arrived, yawning, in the kitchen the next morning.

"Sorry I abandoned you," I said, going to the pot of coffee she'd already made. "And thank you for this life-saving brew."

She laughed. "Hey, you're engaged. I'm sure you were

having a wonderful time with your husband-to-be and lost track of time."

Well, I'd been with Rafe, but last night's activities had been anything but romantic. "Do you want to come to the store this morning and hang out?" I felt bad not being a better host.

She topped her own coffee. "I'm taking a walking tour this morning and then I thought I'd take a bike ride. Everyone here seems to ride."

"Sounds like fun." I wished I could join her, but I had to talk to Violet. "Let's have dinner tonight. We'll go out somewhere fun."

"Sounds good."

Jen was such an easy guest and a fun roommate. I was going to have to carve out more time to spend with her.

I gobbled a quick bowl of cereal, dressed in a light cotton sweater hand-knitted by Theodore in a periwinkle color. I wore it with a white skirt and sandals. I wished Jen a good day and then Nyx and I headed down to work.

When Violet arrived a little later, I studied her carefully. Was her demeanor different? Did she wear the guilt of having killed another witch? Had my assistant committed murder within the last twenty-four hours? She certainly didn't look any more cheerful than she had the last time I'd seen her, but she didn't look like she had blood on her hands, either.

"Feeling better?" I asked, my voice dripping with sarcasm.

She heaved a great sigh. "All right, I was skiving. I admit it. I needed a day off. Besides, I could tell Meri was dying to work in the shop again so she could fawn all over you."

"She does not." Okay, she did a bit. "Anyway, you're changing the subject."

"I didn't know it was a subject. I admitted it. I took a day off. Dock my pay."

"Violet. What did you do yesterday?"

She must have heard something in my tone that was more than mere curiosity.

She looked quite flustered and busied herself with a duster, something she so rarely did that it immediately made me suspicious. I came around in front of her and took the duster out of her hand.

"Violet. I'm serious."

"How about, none of your business?" She looked both defensive and guilty. Never a good combination when you're worried someone's done something bad.

"Please. You can tell me. I'm worried I know what it is anyway."

She took a step back. "Were you spying on me?"

"How could I spy on you when I had a shop to run? Minus one assistant."

"Oh, come on, you can always find a vampire or two to run the shop when you're not here. Anyway, if you didn't spy on me, how on earth could you possibly know what I was doing yesterday?"

"Violet, Karmen is dead."

She blinked at me. "Karmen? Oh, that horrible witch from Wallingford? The one that tried to kill me? Well, if you're looking for tears of sympathy, you won't get them from me."

My tense shoulders began to relax a little. "Are you saying you didn't go there yesterday?"

"Go and see a woman who tried to kill me? Why would I do that?"

"Revenge?"

Then her jaw dropped. "You mean she was murdered?"

I nodded solemnly.

Now her face grew red, and it wasn't embarrassment but fury. "And you think I did it?"

Now it was my turn to look foolish. "Well, if you didn't, why did you look so weird when I asked what you did yesterday?"

"Because I went to talk to William. That's why."

Oh, I felt so stupid now. "You talked to William?" That was good that she was taking my excellent advice. I just wished she'd told me right away, before I accused her of murder. "How did it go?"

She grabbed the duster back, and this time I let her flick it at various surfaces and skeins of wool randomly. She seemed to be redistributing the dust and not getting rid of it. Still, I could tell she needed to spend some of her nervous energy, so I left her flapping the duster around. I'd all but accused her of murder. I supposed a little dust flying around my space was the least I could put up with.

"I couldn't do it, okay? We ended up chatting about your wedding reception, if you must know. He made me taste three kinds of lobster paté. The man sees me and immediately thinks of me as a catering assistant. It's hopeless."

It did sound rather hopeless. "I'm really sorry, Vi."

"Don't be. I'll have to get on with my own life, that's all."

"That's an excellent idea."

She flicked a glance at me. "I was also with your mother. You might as well know that too. No doubt she'll tell you."

Okay, I was still glad she hadn't committed murder yesterday, but hanging out with my mother? I couldn't imagine why. "You promised me there'd be no hen party."

"I'm fairly certain I never technically promised," she said. "Besides, she's your mother. What am I supposed to do? If you don't want a hen party, tell her."

Violet was right. It wasn't fair to make her do my dirty work. "She'll be so disappointed."

"She definitely will. Besides, your mother would hardly drag you around bars and nightclubs until all hours, now would she?"

The thought of my mother on a pub crawl was amusing enough that I sat with the image for a minute or two. "So there's no plan to embarrass me?"

The expression of secret amusement on her face did not convince me. "I'm not giving you any details. The whole point is it's supposed to be a surprise. But you don't need to worry." Then she flicked me another glance. "Too much."

At that moment, my mother called. I sometimes thought her witch senses were active, but unconscious. I'd just been talking about her, and she called. "Lucy," she said, "I need you to come shopping with me."

"Shopping?" My mother was a brilliant archaeologist who cared far more for clothing and personal ornamentation of the Middle Kingdom than she ever cared about her own personal ornamentation. She lived in a uniform of chinos and cotton shirts and boots. She rarely wore makeup and let her hair go. It was so unfair, because she'd been blessed with long, thick, smooth hair, while I had inherited my dad's crazy curls. He wore his cropped close to his head, but I found it easier just to let mine grow and tame the curls with product.

"And," my mother continued, "if I can't buy your wedding dress, then I'd like to buy you a going-away outfit."

"That's so nice of you." I hadn't planned on a going-away outfit. This very simple wedding was getting more complicated by the day. Still, it was nice for Mom and me to bond. She didn't acknowledge that she was a witch, so that whole part of our shared experience was denied us. I had very little interest in Egyptology, so that was another big thing we didn't have in common. We ended up defaulting to things that were not natural to either of us but that we could both tolerate. Like shopping.

Then she said, "And I think we'll get our hair done. I've made appointments for us tomorrow in that darling salon we went to once before."

"Sure. That's a great idea." I'd already asked Sylvia to do my hair for my wedding day. She had a deft touch, and she'd worked with my hair before. I knew I could trust her. But a trim and some shaping before the wedding was probably a really good idea. Mom had clearly not seen the inside of a salon in some time. She had beautiful hair, thick and smooth, and she'd never tried to hide the gray, so it was a pretty salt and pepper but badly in need of styling.

So I agreed that I would meet her at Westgate Shopping Centre the next day.

Nothing out of the ordinary happened all that day. No one died unexpectedly in my presence; the vampires didn't attack any Oxford pedestrians; no magic intervention was needed. Since I was tired from wiping the men's memories and generally on edge, this was a good thing.

Jennifer and I joined Pete and Meri that night for a pub dinner and a nighttime stroll around Oxford.

The next morning, Jennifer said she'd booked a tour of Blenheim Palace and so declined my offer to come shopping. I was a bit sorry, as she made a good buffer between my mother and me, but I was also glad she was making the most of her vacation.

While I was getting ready for my shopping date, my mobile phone rang. It was William. I answered with pleasure and got a crisp voice in reply. I had learned with William that there was off-duty William, who was warm and friendly, and then business-oriented William, who was efficient and clipped on the phone. This was clearly business William. So, not wanting to waste any of his time, I said, "What's up?"

"We're having a bit of an issue with the wedding cake."

"What sort of issue?" I'd given him free rein on the catering, including the cake. How complicated could it be?

He said, "I'd tentatively booked a woman named Poppy Wilkinson, who lives near Bath, to make your cake."

"Bath? That's kind of a long way to go for a wedding cake, isn't it?"

"It is. But she's extraordinary. She went quite far in *The Great British Baking Contest,* and now she bakes all the cakes for the inn at Broomewode. I've seen her work, and her wedding cakes are lovely." There was a slight pause. "And I believe she's one of your kind."

My eyebrows raised, even though he couldn't see me. "My kind? Female? American? Feminist?"

"A witch."

"Oh. That kind. Well, her cake should be magically delicious then."

He didn't seem in the mood for humor. "Now we come to

the sticking point. I've just had a call from Florence Watt. She and Mary want to bake your wedding cake."

"Oh, that is so sweet," I cried. Florence and Mary owned Elderflower Tea Shop next door, and I'd known them since I first began coming to Oxford as a child. They'd been great friends of my grandmother and good friends to me since I'd taken over the knitting shop. "I don't care if you put down a deposit on that other cake. I really think we have to let Florence and Mary make my wedding cake."

He let out a sigh. "I was afraid you'd say that. It won't be as nice as the other, you know."

I looked around to make sure nobody could overhear me. There was only Nyx, and she knew all my secrets. "William, it's not like most of our guests will even taste that cake. And it would mean a lot to me, and my mother, and my friends from Harrington Street."

"Consider it sorted," he said, and then with a curt goodbye was gone.

I wore loose navy cotton trousers that were easy to slip on and off with a white cropped sweater hand-knitted by Clara. When I met up with Mom, I was surprised to find her already pretty dressed up in a floral skirt, silk blouse, and a summer-weight blazer. When I complimented her, she said it was easier to buy dresses when she was already wearing the right underwear and shoes. Good point. I glanced down at my trousers and open-toed black sandals. Oops.

Still, the shopping trip was surprisingly fun.

We started at the hairdresser. They tried to talk Mom into dyeing her hair, but she held firm. I agreed with her decision. Mom was the natural type. She didn't want anything that wasn't super easy care, especially with her lifestyle. I did, however, convince her to let them do our makeup. I was looking for an update on my look for my wedding day, and I thought it might be fun for Mom to have some new cosmetics too. Well, I wasn't actually sure she had any at all. I'd so rarely ever seen her wearing makeup. She argued a bit against it at first, saying she'd just come and watch them do me, but she soon got into the spirit of it.

My hair recognized the hand of a master and decided to behave. After a trim and styling, it looked as good as it ever does, falling in well-behaved curls.

We refreshed ourselves with a quick lunch on the upper floor of Westgate and then braved the shops.

Mom found a gorgeous mother-of-the-bride dress at John Lewis. It was the third outfit she tried, and we both loved it the second we saw her in it. All that digging and the somewhat hard life she lived kept her lean, and when she bothered with her appearance, my mother was a knockout. The dress was fuchsia-colored with a fitted bodice and flared skirt. When she said, "Right, that's done," I dragged her to the shoe section, where we found a pair of Manolo Blahnik sandals with a floral strap and a heel the same color as the dress.

"But they're so expensive," she whispered.

"It's your daughter's wedding," I whispered back. Of course, she bought them. Then turned to me.

"Your turn, Lucy. I want to get you a pretty outfit. Where are you going for your honeymoon?"

That was kind of a sticky point. We'd already had a long vacation, having spent some weeks in New Zealand. Now, I wanted to be around for Gran as she settled into a new life in a new place. No doubt Mom would expect us to choose somewhere exotic but that wasn't going to happen. "We're spending our honeymoon in Cornwall." Even as I said it, I knew that was the perfect destination. Rafe didn't care where we went so he was leaving the choice to me.

My mother's eyes lit up. "You know that's where your father and I had our honeymoon. Oh, Penzance is so wonderful. I'm strongly tempted to extend our trip and come along too."

I couldn't think of a more terrible idea. However, I didn't want to rain on her parade when she was looking so happy and we were having such a nice day. I'd hope Dad could talk her out of going along on her daughter's honeymoon. Somebody had to.

Cornwall was a beautiful part of the world. I imagined Rafe and me walking hand in hand along the cliffside paths and exploring Daphne du Maurier territory. I wasn't above checking out some of the *Poldark* filming sites. Of course, Rafe, being the cultural snob he was, probably didn't even know what *Poldark* was.

More to please her than myself, I tried on a few dresses. I wore so many hand-knitted garments that it almost felt strange to be trying on a store-bought dress. The one I liked best was a sleeveless dress, a navy background with tiny yellow flowers in the print. It had a fitted bodice and loose skirt that hung midway between my knees and ankles. Mom fussed over me and even brought over yellow shoes for me to try on. Dress and shoes fit perfectly and, even if I didn't really need another dress, Mom nodded her head and said to the sales clerk, "We'll take it. And the shoes."

I said, "I'll just go change back into my trousers," but Mom stopped me. "I told your father we'd meet him for a drink after this. Leave the dress on, dear. You look so pretty."

Why not? For once, my mom and I were really getting on well and having a good day.

And so we walked out wearing our brand-new finery, our hair freshly done, and our makeup professionally applied. I caught sight of us in one of the big mirrors and started to laugh. "Look at us. We're like a pair of ladies who lunch."

Her eyes twinkled back at me, but she shook her head. "I'd be so bored. Wouldn't you?"

"You know I would."

"We have that in common, my dear. There's a strong work ethic in our family." She paused. "Maybe I haven't always been as supportive as I could have been about you taking over Cardinal Woolsey's. But I've had a chance to watch you this trip, and I can see how much you enjoy it. And that you're very good at running the business."

This was such rare praise from my mother that I waited for the "but." I waited probably twenty seconds, and it never came. I said, "Wait. Are you saying you finally support my decision to stay and run Cardinal Woolsey's?"

She said, "My darling, I support you in whatever you choose to do. You've chosen a fine man. He has an interesting career, and so do you."

I was so overcome, I threw my arms around her and gave her a hug, which surprised her almost as much as it did me.

Mom glanced at her watch. "Your father should be at the pub now. Won't he be thrilled to see his two best girls looking so pretty?"

I thought my dad would be very unlikely to notice. But I didn't say that.

CHAPTER 13

The cab dropped us off in front of a cocktail bar near the train station that became a noisy night-club when the hour grew later. And I glanced around. This seemed a strange place for Dad to meet us. How did he even know this place was here? It was clearly new since he'd been an Oxford student a million years ago.

"I read about it in one of those online things," my mother said breezily. My mother was not the kind to trawl the internet looking for trendy pubs. I should have realized something was up, but I was still stunned by her sudden support for my business and life plans. My critical faculties were dulled with shock.

I walked in. The place smelled like spilled beer and cheap perfume. This was so not the kind of place my dad would want to come for a drink. Mother seemed oblivious, though. I felt a suppressed excitement in her and imagined she was thrilled to be looking so nice for her husband. I thought it was kind of sweet that she still wanted to pretty herself for him. So I kept my mouth shut. We could have one drink here and move on. We walked in, and instead of going to the front of the pub where there were some tables, Mom kept walking towards the back.

"Where are you going?"

"He said he'd meet us in the back. Come along, dear."

There was no point arguing with her. She was already striding on ahead. I followed as best I could in my unfamiliar new shoes. She pushed open a door and ushered me in ahead of her. There were no lights on, and it was gloomy. Like a party room with no party going on.

"Mom, there's no one—"

Then two things happened at once. All the lights went on, and twenty excited women jumped up and yelled, "Surprise!"

For somebody who supposedly had witch powers, I could not believe how they got me. Mostly, I suppose, because Violet had promised me she wouldn't let Mom organize a hen do. Now, here I was, surrounded by giggling women, trying to put a good face on things.

Violet was doubled over, hanging on to Jennifer and laughing. "Lucy, you should have seen your face."

I gritted my teeth and smiled back at her. "Because it was such a surprise. I wasn't expecting this."

Clearly, she chose to ignore my sarcasm. She rushed up, along with Alice and Scarlett and Polly. "We are going on a hen do to end all hen dos," Violet promised.

Somewhere, a bottle of champagne popped, and then I had a glass in my hand.

"But first, we have to get you properly dressed."

"I am dressed," I told her. And spread my arms so she could see I was in a new dress, new shoes. I looked good. I did not need further ornamentation.

Clearly, my hen party organizers felt differently. From out of a bag came, oh no, the thing I probably dreaded the most. A plastic tiara with a battery pack. Bride, it read, and when Violet pushed the button, which she did with great delight, the word bride flashed on and off. In case anyone might have missed that I was a bride based on the ugliest plastic tiara in the entire world, they also had a Miss America-style sash that said "Going to the Altar" in gold script. Still not happy with their handiwork, they each donned similar tiaras that either said "I'm available" or "Not available," depending on who was married or otherwise hooked up and who wasn't.

What had started out to be a great day was rapidly turning into the worst night of my life.

Scarlett and Polly joined Violet at a table and pulled me over. They spread out a map. "Now, here's our route." And they pointed out every noisy and rambunctious bar, tavern, and pub in Oxford. And there are quite a few of them, given that it's basically a student town.

Oxford might have more genius brain cells per capita than most cities, but a bunch of twentysomethings still know how to party. Not only that, it had somehow become a hub for hen parties and stag parties. I had always sworn I would never inflict one of my own on a beautiful, old city I loved so much.

Apparently, I wasn't going to get my wish.

It was really difficult to pretend to be a good sport when I was seething inside. Bad enough that my mother had wanted to do something crazy to celebrate my upcoming nuptials, but I'd made Violet promise me. Cousin, assistant, sister witch—didn't any of those create a bond strong enough that I could trust her?

Even Jennifer seemed pretty pleased with herself. Wasn't it the part of a bff to warn her closest friend of a do like this? She also wore a pretty dress so either the Blenheim tour had been a ruse or she'd rushed home and changed before coming out to party.

Violet's glee seemed to know no bounds. It flashed across my mind, with the clarity of my flashing tiara, that she might be jealous. Maybe humiliating me like this was a little payback for her, since I had admittedly caught a pretty awesome groom and she couldn't seem to get a second date. But I didn't see how that was my fault or that I should pay such a high price for my good fortune. Even my mother was cackling with glee. Mom just didn't seem like the kind of woman to do shots and ogle male strippers. And based on the way this party was already going, I strongly suspected there were male strippers in my future.

Seriously, if I'd known a disappearing spell, I'd have pulled it out of my bag right then.

Disappearing spell? If I could just tone down the garishness of our display, that would help. It was like every bad cliché of a hen party shoved in my face.

I glanced at my watch. It was still only ten to four. We'd be drunk and falling off our heels before dinnertime.

I decided to be the best sport I knew how to be. At the very least, I could say hello to all these people who'd come out to this terrible idea of a party. I made the rounds, saying hello to some of the students from Cardinal College I'd once worked with during a production. Poor Meri was there, looking bashful and in awe of this display of modern female bonding.

I glanced around and to my surprise saw Jemima Taft in

the corner chatting with Olivia Thresher. I couldn't believe they'd even dragged poor Olivia into this. I hadn't seen Jemima for a while. She was William's financial advisor and I'd come to know her when William catered a dinner for her and some of her extremely wealthy clients, and then she nearly got killed.

"Jemima," I said with pleasure.

"Lucy. I've barely seen you since you saved my life."

I winced, thinking of that terrible time. "It's good to see you."

The server came by with a champagne bottle to top hers up, and she raised a hand. "Just sparkling water for me, thank you."

The Jemima I'd known not so long ago had such a problem with alcohol that she tended to get blotto drunk and blab her clients' secrets. She hadn't even known she was doing it. She looked at me ruefully. "I'm off the booze. One day at a time."

I said, "I think you're doing great. And maybe you can look after the rest of us if we get into an unfortunate condition."

She chuckled at that. "I'll do my best."

Violet and my mother, and even my supposedly best friend Jennifer, were standing together killing themselves laughing. At least somebody was enjoying this humiliation.

Then Mother called out, "Hens, hens, gather all together now. We want to get a picture."

I groaned. The last thing I wanted was a lasting reminder of this. I swore one thing to myself: Rafe was never going to see these photographs.

She got us all into a group and then ran out and dragged

the server back in to take some photographs. They insisted I put on my blinking tiara. We must have looked like the Rockettes in wedding garb.

We started making silly poses, and I couldn't help myself. I started to laugh and got into the spirit of the thing. I was going to be made a fool of anyway. I might as well enjoy it.

Then the moment I'd been dreading arrived. "Okay, let's get ready for the first stop on our itinerary." Violet handed around some party favors. In a barf bag. Laughing, she said, "Make sure you hang on to your vomit bag. Just in case."

I was already feeling queasy just thinking about the evening ahead.

"Right, come on, everybody," Scarlett called out. We piled out of the pub and onto the street, and there was a small tour bus outside. Instead of a destination, it said, "Lucy's Hen Night."

Well, at least they'd thought of everything. Nobody would be drinking and driving. Determined to be a good sport—and if Violet ever got married, to organize her hen night—I got on the bus and sat down. We didn't go far. Instead of pulling up in front of a noisy gin joint, the bus pulled into the sweeping drive of the Wainwright Hotel. It was one of the most exclusive hotels in all of Oxford. I couldn't figure out what was going on.

Mother and Violet turned to me, their eyes dancing with suppressed humor. "You may leave your tiara and vomit bag behind, Lucy. But I will treasure that picture always," Mom said. And then she and Violet fell to laughing so hard, they had to hold each other up in the aisleway of the bus.

Everybody was laughing now, as though they were all in

on the joke. And as they abandoned tiaras, I realized everyone was dressed in some of their nicest finery.

I began to relax. I could even perhaps appreciate that it was a pretty good joke. "So I'm guessing I won't get a private show from a male stripper?"

"Well, we could still arrange it if you wanted one," Violet said.

I put up my hand. "No."

I looked for someone I could trust. Alice. "What's really going on?"

Alice came forward. "It was Jemima who organized it. She has connections here at the Wainwright Hotel. Lucy, we're having afternoon tea."

"Afternoon tea. That's all?" Visions of male strippers and pounding shots danced happily out of my head until Alice shook her head. I groaned. "Wait. Tell me the worst."

"After the tea, we're all having spa treatments."

I burst out laughing. "I can't believe I didn't want a hen party. This is the best idea ever."

$\mathcal{I}$ was having my first fitting for my wedding dress. Naturally, I wasn't standing in a bridal boutique in front of a triple mirror. I was down beneath my shop in the subterranean apartment complex where some of my vampire knitting club members lived. And I could tell they were pretty excited. For some reason, Sylvia and my grandmother had decreed that no male vampires could be present, even though they'd all had a hand in crocheting the dress.

I wasn't going to argue. I thought it would be nice for as many people as possible to be surprised by my gown. So, in spite of some grumbling by Theodore and Alfred, and Christopher Weaver muttering that if he'd known, he wouldn't have worked so hard on the train, they agreed to make themselves scarce while I had my fitting.

I was wearing the pretty new lingerie I had purchased in Paris and never yet worn. It was ivory silk and cost more than my first car. The dress had been put together so beautifully, I couldn't find a seam. When I complimented them, Sylvia said, "Mabel did it. The poor woman has no idea of color, taste, or style, but she's an excellent seamstress. We must give her that."

Mabel didn't look overjoyed by the most backhanded compliment I'd ever heard, but I hastened to thank her for all her meticulous work.

Sylvia also wanted to do a practice run on my makeup and hair, so I arrived with my hair freshly washed but unstyled, my face clean and free of all cosmetics except the day cream I got from Karmen the witch. It did feel strange using her skin cream when she wasn't here anymore, but I had to admit it was beautiful stuff. I wondered if there was anyone who would be able to take over from her. And once again puzzled over who had ended her life.

The media had little to report, only the facts of her death. The police had obviously not shared many details. I would love to delve into the mystery more, and maybe once I was married and back from our honeymoon, I'd have time. Maybe by that time the police would have solved the crime and no one would need my interference. That would be nice.

But for right now, I was not worried about murder. I was much more interested in my wedding gown.

Sylvia set to work, and it was like an undead hen party, as these female vampires I'd grown so close to chatted and giggled while Sylvia expertly did my hair and makeup. Silence Buggins kept trying to tell some boring story about how different weddings were in Queen Victoria's time, but mostly I tuned her out. Hester went dreamy-eyed watching Sylvia get to work. I suspected she was fantasizing about a wedding, perhaps with Carlos.

I'd been absolutely clear I didn't want anything too

formal. It wouldn't suit me. And while I knew she was listening, Sylvia was not a person who gave up her own ideas easily. I suspected I'd get whatever she thought would look good on me, and if I wanted something different, I was going to have to argue my case. However, this was only a practice, so I could relax and enjoy my underground family. We chatted happily, mostly about the move. Sylvia and Gran had been down to Cornwall and just returned.

Gran said, "Wait till you see it, Lucy. It's the most beautiful countryside. And on Rafe's property there's a tin mine that is as nicely set up as our apartments here. There's almost nothing to do but move in. I shall take all my personal effects, of course, but it's perfect. No one knows me there, and I won't be far from you, my dear. You will come and visit very often, won't you?"

I couldn't move my head, as Sylvia was currently putting eyeshadow on my eyelids, so I reached blindly out towards her, and she grasped my hand in her cool one. "I'll visit you as often as I possibly can."

Sylvia said, "You'll want to oversee some redecorating and renovation of the manor house, too. It's a very comfortable bed-and-breakfast, but there have been a great number of tourists through there, and the décor is a little tired. You'll want to turn it back into a family home."

"I can't wait to see it." It was mind boggling to go from someone who lived in a two-bedroom flat above a shop to being married to someone who had more than one manor house. I had no idea of the full extent of Rafe's wealth. I wondered if he even knew it. And I hadn't been in a rush to ask. First, I didn't want him to think I was gold digging, and second, I thought I was going to have to take Rafe's world and life a little at a time. We'd gotten over the biggest hurdle, obviously. I, a mortal witch, was marrying a five-hundred-year-old vampire. Get past that and everything else was going to be easy. Still, I would have to adjust. I mean, the man had a private plane that he never bothered to tell me about until an hour before I got on it. Knowing him, there were houses in other countries, too. I suspected he always needed to know there was a safe place he could escape to.

I wondered if he owned anything in the States. I bet he did.

A few more minutes of smoothing, brushing and penciling, and Sylvia stood back and nodded. "I won't do your lips until you've got the dress on. Heaven forbid you should mar it with a stray smear of lipstick."

Now my genuine excitement turned to nerves. If I mucked up this wedding dress, I might never see my wedding day. I'd witnessed Sylvia angry, and I never wanted to see that again.

"Oh, hush," Gran said to Sylvia. "If she gets a little smear on it, we'll fix it. It's her wedding."

Sylvia merely said, "No reason not to take proper care of things."

Meanwhile, Clara and Mabel had the dress ready. The moonstone buttons gleamed in the soft light as I carefully stepped into the gown. "Did Mr. Herrick do as good a job on recreating the moonstone buttons as the first person who carved them?"

Gran answered. "His are equally as good. He's a real craftsman. We picked up the buttons only yesterday. It was such a thrill."

They'd taken all my measurements, so as I slid my arms into the sleeves, they hugged me but not too tight. The dress felt wonderful. The fine silk thread that had been crocheted with such care whispered against my skin. It was Gran who did each of the tiny buttons up and then, turning me around, took a step back. She clasped her hands together under her chin and said, "Oh, my."

Silence interrupted her own story to say, "You look so beautiful."

Mabel said, "It could have been made for you."

"It was," Sylvia snapped. Never one to gush prematurely, Sylvia took a slow walk all the way around me, stopping to squint behind my left shoulder and then make an infinitesimal shift in the way the fabric sat. She came round to the front and then nodded. "Yes. Perfect."

I let out a breath. I didn't know why I'd been so anxious to please her, but I had. "Can I see?"

For this one night only, they had brought in a mirror. I had no idea where it came from, but it was a proper triple mirror like you'd find in a dress shop. I was dying to go and look at myself, but Sylvia put up a single finger and then went to fetch lipstick. She applied the creamy pink that we'd chosen and then blotted it carefully before standing back once more and giving me a nod. Then she said, "Now you may look."

I trod over to the mirror, and I thought, how did I ever get so lucky? I had the kind of friends who would crochet me a wedding dress and was marrying someone who would love me forever. Above ground, I had slightly eccentric and deranged parents, but I knew they loved me. I had good friends. I had a life. My shop was never going to set the world on fire, but it made a lot of people happy. It made me happy.

I tried not to be vain and was always too quick to note

my own faults, but in that moment, looking at myself in that dress, my hair swept up but still loose and casual and my face made up so that everything looked slightly better than what nature had given me, I felt beautiful. The dress had simple lines. All the fanciness was in the handiwork—the individually crocheted flowers that were as delicate as the finest lace, the train that swept behind me but not so crazy long I'd need three people to hold it up. It was perfect.

Sylvia said from behind me, "Now don't go spoiling that makeup with tears."

That was exactly what I needed to stop me. I burst out laughing. And then I turned and put out my arms, planning to hug each of them in turn, but Sylvia jumped back, horrified, and put her hand up.

"Out of the dress. You're not to touch anything until you're safely out of that dress."

Abashed, I waited while they carefully took me out of the gown, and only then was I allowed to hug them all.

Gran said, "Do you really like it, dear? Because if you don't, we won't be at all hurt. You could go to a boutique and buy something else."

"I could never find anything as beautiful as this. And besides, it was made with love. Every bride should be so lucky."

～

THE NEXT MORNING, I was standing over orders that needed to be mailed out, but my hands were still. I was daydreaming. I saw myself again in that beautiful wedding dress and pictured Rafe's face when he first saw me coming up the aisle. I was pretty sure he was going to approve.

Then I pictured Margaret Twigg standing there, getting ready to marry us, and thought, *What on earth am I going to do?*

She'd probably do a really good job. And, when she wasn't being sarcastic and belittling me, she'd been an excellent mentor and taught me just about everything I knew about being a witch.

Maybe it wouldn't be so bad. As I thought about my wedding day, I wondered if we should have a wedding rehearsal. It was going to be very casual but I wondered if I should get my dad to practice the walk up the aisle since it was going to happen on grass and I didn't want either of us to trip.

Rafe called, and I said, "I was just thinking about you and our wedding."

"That's nice."

I told him about getting Dad to practice walking me down the aisle.

"Good idea, but don't call your father today."

"Why not?"

"He'll be in a delicate condition, I suspect."

"My dad? What happened to him?"

"We had my stag do last night."

I nearly laughed thinking of the vampires and the Egyptologists whooping it up. "You did? What did you do?"

"Lochlan has a business acquaintance who owns a private collection of astonishing quality. Egyptian treasures mainly. Your father was fascinated."

"So fascinated he has a weak head this morning?"

"I suspect that was the brandy."

I chuckled. "Was it here in Oxford?"

"No. Amsterdam."

"You know, when guys head to Amsterdam for a stag party, they don't usually go for the mummies."

"Of course not. Few people in the world will see that collection of antiquities."

So not what I'd meant.

We finished the call and then Nyx jumped up beside me and needed attention. I told her about Margaret Twigg officiating at the ceremony, and she nodded her little chin up and down, though that could have been her way of telling me that she would like to be scratched there. That's usually what that movement meant. While I complied, my phone rang.

"Lucy Swift," I said. I didn't even bother to see who was calling. Between the shop and things for the wedding, I always answered that way these days.

A soft, breathy voice said, "Hello, this is Tilda Ramsay. From Wallingford Botanicals?"

Wallingford Botanicals? What? And then I realized who she was. "Oh, Karmen's assistant. How are you?"

I didn't know what else to say. The poor woman had lost her boss to a violent death. No doubt she was struggling a bit. Was she even still employed?

"I'm all right. Thank you for asking. I wanted to let you know that your bridesmaid gifts are ready."

"Oh, right." I had completely forgotten about them in all the chaos. "Where should I come and pick them up?"

"I'm still operating the business. If you'd like to come to Wallingford, you can pick them up there. Or I'd be happy to drive them to Oxford for you. I know it's what Karmen would want me to do." Her voice trembled at the end, on the edge of tears. I hastened to assure her that it was no problem at all for me to come up to Wallingford.

It wasn't only that I didn't want to put the poor woman out of her way, but I hadn't done a single thing about trying to solve the murder of a woman who had sent me a deadly gift. There was something very strange going on, and as Rafe had reminded me, Karmen might have tried to murder me, but someone else had much more successfully done the job on her.

Solving one murder might prevent a second one.

Mine.

Planning a wedding was all very well, but I'd quite like to survive long enough to actually walk down the aisle, especially now I had that beautiful dress.

It might have been shallow, but those really were the thoughts going through my mind at that moment. Nyx, obviously sensing that my attention had wandered, ceased purring and gave an annoyed *brrp* and then stalked off to the front shop.

On impulse, I called Rafe. He picked up on the first ring.

"Lucy," he said, his voice filled with pleasure. "Did you speak to your father?"

"No. I'll wait until he's recovered."

"A sound plan."

I told him that Tilda had just called to say she had bridesmaid gifts ready for pick up. "I was thinking, if we went together, we could look around a little. I could keep her chatting while you poked into corners to see if there are any clues to what happened to Karmen."

"That's an excellent idea. Can you give me half an hour to finish up here and then I'll come and fetch you?"

"Perfect." That would give me time to get my mind out of the clouds and finish packing up the orders.

When I went back out front to tell Violet the bad news, that I was actually going to leave her alone for a couple of hours, my mother was coming in the front door.

"Hello, girls. Wasn't that the most glorious tea?"

"It was. And the massage I had was amazing," I said. "I didn't know how tense I was."

Mom flashed her manicure at us. "It's such a treat to have pretty nails. Not very practical for my work, of course, but so pretty for your wedding."

Violet showed off her pedicure. Her purple toenails were very pretty, but I'd assumed she'd chosen a facial, since her skin looked so dewy and fresh. I moved closer to her, pretending an interest in her pedicure, and by concentrating, picked up a faint but familiar scent.

"And I've been having the most wonderful morning at my old college," my mother said. "Quite a walk down memory lane."

I told Mom I had to run soon, and she didn't seem to mind. "I can keep Violet company then."

"Right. Could you excuse me and Violet for a few minutes? I need to show her something upstairs."

Violet looked surprised, since I never took her upstairs for work chats, but Mother didn't know that and said she could certainly manage to hold the fort. "Perhaps I should take up knitting," she said, picking up one of the newest magazines.

I ushered Violet upstairs. She appeared uncomfortable, a

little nervous even, when I didn't offer her a seat and stood there with my arms crossed.

"Where's Jennifer?" she asked, looking around.

"She's at Crosyer Manor helping Olivia plan the garden decorations." I loved how quickly Jennifer had jumped into her bridesmaid role, and she and Olivia had bonded at my hen party. I'd worried that she'd be bored, but between sightseeing and helping with wedding prep, she was as busy as I was. Also, not here to shield Violet. "I know you're wearing face cream from Wallingford Botanicals, so don't even try to deny it."

"So what?" she said, trying to brazen it out.

I was coldly furious. "So you lied to me. You went there that day, didn't you? You went to see Karmen. And yet when I asked you, you claimed you'd been to see William."

Her color fluctuated from red to white and back again. "I did go to see William that day."

Then she looked down at her purple toes peeking from her sandals. "But, okay, I also went to see that witch."

"On the day she died." I didn't know how bad it was, but I didn't have a good feeling about this.

Vi glanced up at me and snapped, "I didn't know she was going to die."

Had she had something to do with it? I didn't want to accuse her, as she might stomp back downstairs and hide behind my mother. I could tell she was thinking about it. I forced myself to relax and tried to sound calm. "Tell me what happened."

She let out a breath, obviously trying to calm herself. "It was Margaret Twigg's idea."

Why was I not surprised? "Go on."

"There's not much to tell. I went to see Margaret and told her you'd seen Karmen and that she'd admitted to selling the hex. Margaret said we had to stop her from selling her wares in Oxford and harming another witch. She was angry, and you know how Margaret gets when she's angry."

I nodded. I did. But I'd never seen her murderous. "What did Margaret do?"

"We drove out to Wallingford together...that day."

"The day Karmen died."

"Quit rubbing it in. We didn't know she was dying, and we had nothing to do with it."

"You just dropped in for tea?"

"No need to be sarcastic. No. Margaret told her she'd nearly killed me and what did she have to say for herself."

I wondered if Karmen had treated Margaret to the same blasé attitude I'd been subjected to and doubted it.

"Karmen said she hadn't known it was meant for one of her sisters, and while she never said she was sorry, she did give both me and Margaret a jar of her special recipe face cream." She touched her cheek. "I wasn't going to use it, but you'd raved about it, so I tried it, and I can already see the difference in my skin." She shook her head. "I wish she hadn't died. Now what will we do when we run out?"

She looked at me like this was a serious question. "Never mind that. When were you there?"

Now she looked at me sheepishly. "We passed you on the road."

"We?" I'd seen Margaret in the car but no passenger.

"I saw the car coming toward us. I felt your energy, so I ducked down so you wouldn't see me."

"Why didn't you tell me this before?"

"I don't know. You practically accused me of killing the witch, and I hadn't, so I didn't tell you I'd been at her cottage."

"How did she seem? Was she ill? Was anyone else there? You may have been the last people to see her before I found her on the floor dying."

She shook her head. "We weren't the last. That man was."

CHAPTER 15

I could cheerfully have slapped my cousin. "What man?"

"How should I know? A man. He was coming toward her cottage as we were leaving."

"What did he look like?"

"A man. Middle-aged. Not remarkable in any way."

"Tall? Short? Dark hair? Light?"

"Tall, I think. And I couldn't see his hair. He wore a cap." She tapped her foot. "And to answer your question, Karmen said she'd offer us tea but she wasn't feeling well. She was going to lie down."

"So you took your face cream and left."

"Yeah."

Before I could ask anything else, she said, "We can't leave your mother in the shop alone." And ran down the stairs.

While I was in my flat anyway, I fussed with my appearance. Okay, it was super vain of me, but I changed my top for a prettier one and did the best I could with my hair and brushed my teeth and refreshed my makeup. I was a bride-to-be about to spend time with her fiancé. I was allowed to fuss a little. No doubt the day would come when Rafe would find me slopping around in my old sweats, my hair unkempt and my socks unmatching. But that day had yet to dawn.

This also gave me a few minutes to calm down and sift what Violet had shared. Naturally, it would have been very helpful if she'd shared this information earlier. She'd passed a possible murderer. Had Tilda seen this person? Did the police know about his visit?

When I got back to the shop, Vi and my mother were giggling over something.

Even though I was annoyed with my cousin, I still thought it was cute that these two had bonded over my hen party. They were relatives, but, because of the falling out between Gran and my great aunt Lavinia, the two families had never spent much time together. I'd never even known I had a cousin. Violet avoided all conversation about witchcraft with my mother. I wasn't entirely sure what they found to talk about, but they seemed to chat away like old friends. And they certainly enjoyed ganging up to tease me.

Violet clearly wanted to make nice, as she told me she'd finish packing the mail orders for me and would even take them to the post office and mail them.

"And don't worry about leaving the shop, Lucy," Mom said. "I'll spend the afternoon here. I can help if any customers come in."

This was so different from the mother I used to know. She'd suddenly become quite supportive of Cardinal Woolsey's. It probably wouldn't last, but it was a relief not to field her constant suggestions for better career choices. I said goodbye to them both when Rafe's car pulled up in front and ran out to join him.

On the way to Wallingford, he told me about how William was driving him mad turning the manor house and gardens into a wedding venue. "He seems to have forgotten that it's also my home."

I bit my lip to keep from laughing out loud. Rafe had wanted to get married there as much as I had. I suspected pre-wedding jitters and was charmed.

And then I told him about Violet and Margaret Twigg visiting Karmen the day she'd died. He wasn't as concerned as I was that the police didn't know about this mysterious tall man in a cap who'd come to call, but then he'd seen a lot more of the world—and death—than I had.

Soon we were pulling up into the drive that led to the old pub and Karmen's cottage. A cold shiver ran down my spine as we pulled up and the memory of her awful death came back to me, as sharp and clear as when I'd seen her transformed into an old woman, dying in front of me.

"And the police have no leads?" I asked him. He always knew. He had contacts everywhere.

He hesitated, looking worried. "She died of arsenic poisoning. I wasn't going to tell you until after our wedding."

"Arsenic poisoning," I repeated, thinking back to the rune box and the "present" it contained. I didn't want to think someone was out to kill Karmen and me. "Could she have made a bad batch of her elixir?"

"I don't think so. There was too much arsenic to have been an error."

Great. "Well, maybe if you look around today, you'll see something the police have missed."

He didn't look convinced, but he nodded. "Perhaps."

We got out and headed to the pub. I knocked on the door and Tilda opened it. She looked as though she'd been recently crying. "I would have brought your things to you. You must have such a lot on your plate, getting married."

But she held the door wide, and we both walked in. Her eyes widened slightly when she saw Rafe. She must have been remembering the last time she'd seen him, that awful day when her employer died. All I said was, "You remember Rafe? He's my fiancé. He drove me here."

Oh, Lucy, how many more times can you fit the word "fiancé" in during one day?

She said, "Congratulations," to him. Then to me, she said, "I have your bridesmaid gifts over here. I thought you might like to look at them before we package them up. Just to make sure everything's perfect."

"That's a great idea," I gushed, not because I thought she'd made any mistakes but so Rafe could wander around for a few minutes undisturbed. I doubted there was too much here in the pub where Wallingford Botanicals' business was run. No doubt we'd have to come back under cover of darkness and have a good snoop around her house. There was no sign of police activity, so presumably they'd finished their forensic investigation.

In spite of her grief, Tilda had done a perfect job. The cloth bags were beautifully sewn, and the names embroidered on the front. I doubted I'd be giving my bridesmaids these gifts now, though. What if they were "accidentally" laced with arsenic too? I couldn't take the chance. I wanted to keep Tilda talking for a few minutes while Rafe snooped around, so I asked her whether she'd be staying on.

"I think so. I hope so, but that depends on her husband. He inherits everything."

"Her husband?" This was news. There'd been no trace of a man in Karmen's home. "I had no idea she was married."

"They haven't been together for years. Patrick Herrick runs a crystal shop in town. I've asked him to think about keeping the business going. I could run it myself if I hired a helper. He said he'd think on it."

I tried to keep my expression neutral, but Patrick Herrick could easily fit Violet's description of the man who'd visited Karmen as they were leaving on the day she died. Perhaps, while we were here, we might pay Herrick's Crystal a visit.

There was no sign of Rafe in the main room. He was in the kitchen studying one of the stenciled sayings. "These are interesting," he said as we came into the kitchen. "Were they here in the old days at the pub?"

There was no way those stencils were that old, and if I knew it, he definitely knew it. He must have been trying to get some information out of Tilda. Obligingly, she walked closer to him.

"I don't think so. I've always assumed that Karmen put them there. They're in Latin, aren't they? I don't know what they mean. Never thought to ask Karmen."

"Interesting," he said again. And then looked at me. "Ready to go?"

I nodded, and we left.

I waited until we were driving away to ask, "Well? Did you find anything?"

"Only that saying stenciled on the wall."

"My Latin's a little rusty. What did it say?"

"Essentially, from the cygnet comes the swan."

"Hardly a revelation. A cygnet's a baby swan, right? And it grows into a swan?"

"It's also associated with alchemy."

Now that was interesting. "Really?"

"Yes. And that symbol that was beside the stenciled saying but down below a little bit. That's the symbol for arsenic." I remembered the symbol. It was a triangle with the sharp point facing down and a shape like the letter A without its crosspiece over top, and a tiny squiggle trailing off the right side of the open A. Who decorated their walls with symbols denoting a deadly poison?

Now I felt as though I'd dipped my feet into ice water. "Arsenic killed Karmen."

"And arsenic almost killed you, if you'd taken that substance that was in the box with the runes."

He didn't need to remind me. "And the message on the box, 'As above, so below,' also refers to alchemy, right?"

"Yes."

"But I don't understand. Why would she have the alchemical symbol for arsenic on her wall?"

"Arsenic is a powerful symbol of alchemy itself. Arsenic in its raw state is a dull white color, but when heated, it changes color."

"But still, it's a strange thing to put on her wall."

"There were a lot of strange things on her wall. I had a few minutes to study the various sayings while you two were busy. They all relate to alchemy in some way, but there are snippets of various ideas and concepts. She had quotes stretching from Isaac Newton to Carl Jung."

"Do you think she just stenciled things that interested her? Maybe the arsenic symbol appealed to her visually."

"It's possible, but I don't think so. Like all alchemists, I suspect Karmen was very secretive. Everything was in code."

"And so you think if we could crack the code, we might figure out who killed her?"

"If we could crack the code, we might find her recipes."

"Do you really need a recipe to turn lead into gold?" I asked it a bit sarcastically. That man did not need any more wealth.

He looked at me in surprise. "No. I want to stop that recipe from falling into the wrong hands."

I shuddered at the idea of the wrong person pretty much having an endless supply of gold. They could seriously screw up international markets, build armies. I could think of a lot of things somebody with evil intent and a lot of money could do. I understood why he wanted to make sure we got there first. Except that I didn't think she'd been turning out gold. "Rafe, I think she'd found the elixir of youth, not a way to make gold."

He turned to look at me. "Yes. Exactly. Imagine such a formula in the possession of someone with evil intent."

Like, for instance, her murderer.

"Maybe whoever killed Karmen already has what they were looking for."

"It's possible, but I don't think so."

"Why?"

He shook his head. "Instinct. Some things I can't explain, I just sense."

I nodded. It was something I understood well and was only beginning to really listen to in my own life. I'd ignored that little voice of wisdom too many times, and now I was trying to treat it with the respect it deserved. And what was that little voice trying to tell me now? I closed my eyes and went back to that scene in the pub.

"Do you think Tilda knows anything?"

"Not to be rude, but one glimpse of Tilda's aging complexion and I would say no."

"Can we make a stop in town? I want to visit the crystal shop." Then I told him what Tilda had shared, about Karmen being married to Patrick Herrick, who owned the shop. I couldn't tell Rafe about the moonstone buttons with the tiny suns and moons carved into them, but they were symbols of alchemy too. Alchemy was suddenly everywhere.

"I think that could be the guy Violet saw when she and Margaret Twigg were leaving Karmen's house that day."

"Her description was so vague, it would fit any number of middle-aged men."

"True, but how many of them were married to Karmen?" I shifted in my seat. "Besides, I can't give my bridesmaids these creams now. What if they're laced with arsenic? But there were some very pretty bracelets in Herrick's Crystal."

"Fine." Rafe found a place to park, and we walked up to the crystal shop.

Fortunately, Patrick Herrick was alone in his shop with a newspaper spread out on the top of his display counter. If he recognized me, he gave no sign. I was so happy he didn't say, 'So, did those moonstone buttons work out for your wedding dress?' as I wanted every piece of my dress to be a surprise to Rafe. "Afternoon. Looking for anything special?"

"Yes." I went to a lovely sterling silver bracelet with an aquamarine set into it. "I want to buy four of these but each with a different stone. Could I have them within a week?"

"If I've got the stones, I don't see a problem."

"Wonderful. I had planned to give my bridesmaids gifts from Wallingford Botanicals, but now that Karmen's dead..." I petered out, watching him carefully. His gray eyes sharpened, but he only said, "Very sad business."

"You were married to her, I understand."

"Not for years." He picked the bracelet out of the display case. "What stones were you thinking of?"

"Serpentine for a woman who loves to garden. It's a stone that connects to nature." Even though Olivia wasn't a bridesmaid, I wanted to get her one of the bracelets.

He nodded, found me some, and I chose a piece that was the color of moss with streaks of yellow through it.

"For my friend who's expecting her first child, I thought red jasper."

He nodded. "The nurturer. Excellent choice."

Then, with great casualness, while I perused the stones, I said, "I really like the Wallingford Botanicals creams. Will you keep the company going?"

"Don't know yet."

For Violet, I thought jet, good for scrying and intuition, and it was grounding. Plus, she wore a lot of black.

My eye kept going back to the aquamarine bracelet. I'd been undecided about what to get Jennifer amid a huge life transition. Jade for good luck? Opal for magic and visions? But really aquamarine was a go-with-the-flow kind of stone. Good for clarity, which would be perfect for someone going through a transition. And it was so pretty. I could see the aquamarine bracelet on Jen's wrist.

Having made my choices, I took out my card to pay. "When will Karmen's funeral be held? I'd like to attend. I didn't know her well, but we were friendly."

As he rang up my purchase, he said, "Police haven't released her body yet. I'll warn you now, she specified a woodland burial. Never mind that she's got a ruddy great mausoleum in her back garden." The irritable way he discussed her final arrangements very much sounded like an ex-husband.

A woodland burial was a popular choice for a witch, easing her earthly body back into nature. As above, so below.

He said he'd let me know when he had a date for the ceremony, though I rather thought I'd find out through the coven. I was to come back in four days, and he'd have the bracelets ready.

Once we were back in the car, I asked Rafe, "Do you think he killed his ex-wife?"

"Not ex, apparently. It sounds like they never bothered to get divorced."

"That old pub and the cottage and land it's on must be worth quite a bit," I said.

"Enough to murder a former wife over?"

And wasn't that the question?

CHAPTER 16

As we drove back to Oxford, I said, "If Patrick Herrick killed Karmen, he didn't do it for her youth formula, based on how old he looks."

"I agree. If the killer's got hold of the elixir of youth, I imagine they're using it."

"So we're looking for somebody with unnatural, youthful good looks and very nice skin tone." I glanced at him. "Who doesn't happen to be a vampire."

"I would say so."

"Where are we going to find them? People who are actually, genuinely young are going to look like that."

"Nobody said it would be easy. And Karmen, like many an alchemist before her, did everything she could to obscure her path."

"You don't think she obscured it completely?"

"It would be unusual. She had to be able to recreate her recipe. Possibly pass it on. No, I expect it's well hidden. No doubt she has a workshop, too, also well hidden." After a while he said, "We need to search her house and property."

I'd known we would get here, but still I shied away. "Rafe, what if we get caught? We're getting married in a week. I don't want to postpone the wedding because one or both of us is in jail."

"It won't come to that," he said with confidence.

I wasn't so sure. Besides, I actually wanted to plan my wedding, not spend the next week digging around for musty old alchemy secrets. I had Jennifer to entertain and our shared discovery that we were both witches to explore further.

I'd have gone back home with Rafe, but of course I had a house guest. So I got him to drop me off at my flat. "Try not to worry," he said, kissing me goodnight.

I'd try, but I doubted I'd succeed. I went upstairs feeling tired and unsettled, but at least I had the bridesmaids' gifts sorted out.

As I walked into my flat, my nose picked up a mingling of scents that immediately transported me back to my childhood. The nose can be as good as a wand at casting a spell and sending you back into the past.

Immediately, my mood lightened. Yes, Karmen was still dead. And yes, something very strange was going on and I might even be in danger. But Jennifer was here, and I smelled popcorn and hot chocolate. I ran the rest of the way up the stairs and found her in the living room.

She said, "Oh good. I was afraid I'd started the popcorn too early." She gave me a searching look. "Are you okay?"

I flopped down on the couch beside her. "Better now."

"I'm sure you have a million things to do, but just for tonight, we're going back in time."

I liked this idea already. "Let me change into my sweats. I'll be right back."

I ran upstairs and washed my hands and face thoroughly, just in case anything had attached to me from an alchemist's workshop where she kept the symbol of arsenic prominently on the wall. I came back down, and I swear my tread was lighter, as though I were thirteen again. On the table in front of the couch were two huge bowls of popcorn, laden with butter exactly the way we both liked it. Beside that was a bowl of mixed American candies that made me laugh out loud.

"Peanut butter cups? Hershey's Bars. And are those gummy worms?"

"You bet. All the things we used to love as kids. I've even got licorice."

"This is so awesome," I said, even sounding like I was back in the nineties.

She went to the small kitchen and poured two big mugs of hot chocolate from a saucepan she'd had heating on the stove. "I could have done this by magic, but it was more fun to do it the old-fashioned way." She popped marshmallows on top of the hot chocolate and came over.

We both put our feet up on the coffee table and grabbed a bowl of popcorn and a tea towel.

"Are you ready for my surprise?"

"There's more?"

She laughed, turned on the TV, and there was an episode of *Friends* playing. "I had to do a compilation for you. I was going to just play the episodes where they go to London for Ross's wedding, but he never actually marries that girl. It seemed like bad luck."

I couldn't believe how much effort she'd gone to. "This is

going to be so much fun." And so, for one evening, I didn't think about alchemy or witches or even wedding planning. I turned my phone off, settled back with my best friend in the world, and chomped popcorn and traveled back in time. At the end of two hours, we were both sniffling a little bit as the cast of *Friends* said goodbye to their apartment.

She said, "I can't believe how quickly time is passing. Lucy, we're going to be thirty."

"I know. I thought I'd know who I was by now."

"Well, we know a lot more than we did when we watched this show."

This was true. Though life had been much simpler life back then, when marrying Chandler had been the sum total of my hopes and dreams in life. Jennifer had always been more Team Joey, so we didn't even have conflict in that department. In fact, it was scary how compatible we were. Of course, now it made more sense. We'd probably been unconsciously using our magic all the time. I bet when there'd been a movie I'd wanted to see and she hadn't and then suddenly she'd changed her mind, I'd unconsciously manipulated her. And when she wanted Ugg boots and I claimed they were too expensive, we suddenly found ourselves at the store buying matching pairs of Ugg boots in slightly different colors. She'd probably cast a spell on me. Ha.

"Don't forget we're shopping for bridesmaid dresses tomorrow," I reminded her.

She groaned and grabbed her stomach. "I forgot. You never should have let me eat all that junk food. We'll have to get up early and jog." And both swearing we'd jog tomorrow, which we'd also used to say when we were thirteen and very rarely did, we both went upstairs to bed.

CHAPTER 17

Saturday morning Jen and I both forgot about the jogging. Scarlett and Polly arrived in plenty of time to take over Cardinal Woolsey's. I'd made an appointment at a local bridal shop where the woman who owned it promised she had enough dresses in stock that she could have any alterations done in plenty of time. "Though you have left it a bit late," she chided. I knew a week wasn't a long time in the world of wedding planning, but I'd wanted to wait until the bridesmaids could go shopping together.

We met at the bridal boutique, and all of us were in a happy mood, even Violet.

Tara, who ran the shop, was about my age, and within five minutes of arriving, I knew we'd come to the right place. She was dressed stylishly, and her gowns were beautiful.

She asked about the venue, and Jen, brilliant friend that she was, pulled out her phone and showed Tara photos of the garden and veranda of Rafe's house.

"What a stunning location," Tara said in a posh girl accent. "I do love a garden wedding."

I showed her a photograph of my dress, and she praised the handiwork and said the style was perfect on me. Which was nice, seeing that she was in the business. "Right," she said, "I'm going to pull out a few things that I think will suit all of you and look lovely with Lucy's dress."

She and an assistant brought three gowns into the front showroom: a patterned floral dress with a sweetheart neckline, a long dress in lavender with short sleeves, and a pale green sleeveless column, also floor-length.

I knew immediately which one I liked, but looked at the others, waiting for their opinions.

"I like the green one," Vi said.

"Me too," Jen agreed.

"It's my favorite, too, but what about the tummy?" Alice asked, then explained in a shy but very proud voice that she was expecting.

"Let's try them on and see," the very practical Tara suggested. "Why don't you all try the green one on and we'll go from there."

"I'm a size six," Jen announced.

"Not in the UK, you're not," Tara informed her, handing her a dress.

She eyeballed both the other women and handed them dresses, too. Oh, she was good.

I sat in a plush chair surrounded by mirrors and waited as the three bridesmaids went into the changing rooms.

When they came out in the green dresses, they all looked amazing. There was a slight sideways sweep of fabric across the waist that hid Alice's barely-there pregnancy and was flattering to the other two. They preened and looked critically at their back views, and then the three of them stood together. "What do you think?"

"I think you all look beautiful." They did, too. The color flattered all of them and the dresses were simple and classic.

They tried on the other two dresses simply to confirm that the first choice had been the right one, but we all agreed that the green was the winner. There were a few alterations to be done, but they were all slight, and Tara promised the dresses would be ready by Wednesday. That left days to spare before my wedding.

That done, we headed in search of shoes and ended up with silver sandals that Alice picked out and all of us loved.

After that, naturally we went out for lunch. It was nice for Jen to get better acquainted with Alice and Violet, and I was happy to see that Violet was in good form. I suspected she'd needed to feel more a part of the wedding.

We lingered over coffee, and then Alice said she had to get back. Violet had some other shopping to do, so that left Jen and me. "Do you want to go somewhere?" I asked, thinking I could take her sightseeing.

"What I'd really like to do is head to Rafe's house. Now that we have the bridesmaid dresses picked out, Olivia and I need to choose ribbons and make certain all the flowers and plants still work."

I loved how seriously Jen was taking her duties, plus I was happy to spend the afternoon at Crosyer Manor. It was a beautiful afternoon, and I was certain William would have questions for me.

I called to let Rafe know we were on our way, and by three, we were pulling into the drive. "Every time I come here,

I feel like I'm about to step into a British costume drama," Jen said, already reaching for Henri's treat.

We spent a busy afternoon planning things like lighting for the wedding reception when the sun went down, and while William ran over a million details with me, Jen and Olivia worked on décor.

Rafe came in and out, looking distracted. Lochlan came in at one point carrying his briefcase. Rafe had put him in the guest wing, as he was doing business in Oxford and London while he was here.

I finally followed Rafe into his study to find him puzzling over the spellbound alchemy book. "No luck?" I asked. "Maybe the spell has to come off first."

"But the book's perfectly legible. My guess is the book works on two levels."

"Like alchemy?" I asked him. "As above, so below."

"Exactly." He pushed the book away. "And this witch's death is bothering me, too. The police have precious few leads in the case."

I had an idea. "Rafe, what if we call a special meeting of the vampire knitting club? Not a regular knitting meeting but one where we got a bunch of different brains working on the puzzle of Karmen's death."

"That's not a bad idea. I'm certainly out of ideas. Lochlan's got a good head for that sort of thing, too."

I didn't want to hold it in the back room of my shop as usual, because Mom had a habit of arriving at my place whenever she felt like it. What if she came to call on me upstairs? And I was in the back room with a bunch of vampires, including her own mother? I didn't think that would go over well. We were getting on so well doing all this wedding planning, I didn't want to ruin a good thing.

"We'll have it here," Rafe said. He looked quite pleased by the idea. "Tonight?"

I put up my hands. "I don't have any other plans. And Jen will get to meet the other vampires."

Lochlan and Jen both said they were in, so Rafe organized it with the other vampires. This wasn't the first time we'd met at his place, and it was easily accomplished. As many as could pile into the Bentley did, and Carlos, the Cardinal College student who had become friendly with Hester, also brought some of the vamps in his car.

Naturally, even though we were here for sleuthing, everybody still had their knitting. Including Jennifer. I had a partially completed winter scarf that I'd left at Rafe's, so I unenthusiastically pulled that out.

I introduced her to everyone, and she sat next to Gran. They seemed delighted with each other and chatted away until the meeting began.

Lochlan didn't knit, so he manned the whiteboard. He seemed very accustomed to doing that. I supposed a guy who ran a high-tech firm was pretty used to scribbling stuff on whiteboards—though hopefully, not very often clues to a murder.

He started out by putting the dead witch's name on the top. Karmen Herrick. "What do you know about her?" he asked aloud, and as we called out ideas, he wrote down in bullet points:

- Alchemist, looked much younger than her actual age.

192

- Called the Wicked Witch of Wallingford. (Gran couldn't help herself.)
- Died of arsenic poisoning.
- Last words "The book."
- Ran Wallingford Botanicals.

I had printed off the pictures that I'd taken of those stenciled slogans in her kitchen, and we passed them around.

When they got to Jennifer, she looked very closely before saying, "Rafe, do you have any alchemy books? What do the rest of the symbols look like?"

Naturally, Rafe had loads of books on alchemy, probably every one ever printed. He brought her out a selection, including the one he'd mysteriously acquired, and while the meeting went on, I watched Jennifer flip through one after another. I suspected she had something in mind and she'd speak up when she had something to say.

She came at last to that strange new/old spellbound book, and when there was a pause, Jennifer said, "I think I might have found something."

Naturally, we all turned to her. She looked at Lochlan. "Do you mind?" And then she rose and came forward. He happily passed her the pen for the dry-erase board, and she drew the arsenic symbol.

Then she drew a second one. I wasn't sure where she was going with this.

It was Theodore who said, "They aren't the same." Trust an artist to have that kind of eye to detail.

"They aren't?" I asked. I couldn't see the difference.

She nodded her head and nodded to him as though he were a prize pupil in her class. "Exactly. Look at this." And she circled a squiggle at the bottom of the arsenic symbol that had been stenciled on the wall of Karmen's workshop kitchen. And then she opened the mysterious alchemy book, and there was the same squiggle. "But in regular alchemy books, the symbol for arsenic doesn't have that extra codicil."

"That's very clever of you, dear," Gran said, as proud as though Jen was another granddaughter.

She nodded, looking pleased with herself. I passed the book around, my chest swelling with pride. Jennifer was my best friend for a reason. And the vampires who'd definitely been a little uncomfortable having yet another mortal amongst them immediately warmed up to her. I could see that by the end of the evening, she'd be an honorary member of the club too. I mean, unlike me, she could actually knit.

Rafe said, "Well done, Jennifer." He was always generous with praise when somebody got something right.

"But what does it mean?" Hester asked, looking aggrieved by the whole process. I thought she was just annoyed that she hadn't figured out the connection.

"I think it means," Jennifer said, "that the Wicked Witch of Wallingford owned this book. And I'm going to take a huge step forward here and suggest that she's the one that put the spell on it." She tapped the word "book" on the whiteboard. "And this is what she was referring to when she cried 'the book,' the last words she spoke before she died." Jen turned to Rafe. "Did she know it was in your possession?"

"I'm beginning to think she was the one who sent it to me," Rafe said.

"If we can break the spell of this book, we may figure out who murdered her."

There was silence in the room as we all took this in.

"But how are you going to break that spell?" Gran asked. "It looked very tightly locked to me."

I had an idea. "We were able to turn back a hex that Karmen witch put on Violet. It was the combined power of me, Violet, my great-aunt Lavinia and"—here I felt my voice hitch—"and Margaret Twigg, the head of our coven."

Jennifer nodded as though it was a good idea. "So the combined power of the right energy might just be enough to break the spell."

"I think so. Maybe."

"I still don't understand why that witch tried to kill Lucy with a poisoned elixir of life sent to her in a box decorated with runes," Gran said.

Jennifer wrote on the board, *As above, so below.* "That was the basic message of the runes, correct?"

Rafe agreed that it was.

She tapped the pen against the saying. "That's one of the most important slogans in alchemy, and it was the message on the rune box."

We all looked at her, waiting for the next part, but she seemed like she'd run out of steam.

Rafe continued, "And the swan is often used as a symbol for arsenic in alchemy."

I felt a jolt of excitement. "From the cygnet, comes the swan. Another stenciled saying on her wall. Are they clues? Like a treasure hunt?"

Sylvia had been watching all of this with cynicism, I thought. Meanwhile, she was busily knitting. But suddenly she put her knitting down and said, "I don't give a flying fig who killed that woman. But I paid an extremely high price to buy Lucy enough of the elixir of life to keep her young and beautiful for centuries. That's all I care about. So where's this woman's recipe book? Where's the elixir she took for however long she's been alive? That's what I want to know."

Lochlan nodded. "We should probably get hold of her alchemist's laboratory. If she successfully managed to make the elixir of life, then you're right. It shouldn't fall into the wrong hands."

"As above, so below. Did she have swans?" Gran asked.

Sylvia suddenly put her knitting away and stood up. "I don't know about you, but I feel that there's no time like the present. We'll need shovels and some good strong backs. Somewhere in that witch's house or on her property, we will find that elixir. Who's with me?"

Jennifer turned and stared at me with a startled gaze. I shrugged. I was too accustomed to Sylvia to be surprised. Besides, what seemed like time to go to bed for us was when the vampires were at their most energetic.

"Sounds like an excellent idea," Carlos said. "I have a strong back. I don't mind doing some digging."

Once the young, sexy Spaniard had spoken, all the vampires agreed that they also had strong backs and could think of nothing they'd rather do than dig up a witch's garden in Wallingford in the middle of the night.

Rafe looked at me inquiringly, and I nodded. I didn't think I'd get any sleep tonight anyway. We might as well take a field trip.

He said, "Olivia will have gone to bed now, but there are shovels and every gardening tool you could imagine in the outbuildings. Help yourselves."

Carlos led everyone out. Only my gran and Sylvia stayed

behind. I hadn't thought that Sylvia would be the one to get her hands dirty. She was more management than labor.

"Do you think she really did have the elixir of life?" Jennifer asked.

Sylvia nodded.

"Wow. That would be cool," Jennifer said.

I nodded.

"And possibly dangerous," Jennifer reminded us. "I was looking through those alchemy books. A lot of their recipes contained arsenic in small quantities." She put up her hands. "And I think most of them didn't work."

"If Karmen's elixir kept her alive well past her natural span, a little arsenic can't have done her much harm," Sylvia said, finishing a row.

Lochlan said, "It's all about balance."

"You don't have to come with us," I said to Jennifer. "You must be so tired."

She looked at me. "Are you kidding? I wouldn't miss it."

So we decided that everyone would go in the same car as they arrived at Rafe's in, except that Jennifer and I would go with Rafe in his Land Rover and Lochlan would ride along with us. Unfortunately, the noise and commotion of several vampires helping themselves to the tools out of her gardening shed woke Olivia, who stumbled out, looking understandably annoyed.

When she heard what was going on, she first of all wanted to come along with us, but Rafe said there were too many people coming already.

When Alfred and Theodore and Hester arrived with various digging implements, some of them with earth clinging to them, Sylvia freaked out. "I'm not having all that dirt in the Bentley."

Olivia, sleepy as she was, managed a chuckle. "Why don't you borrow my truck?"

That turned out to be a fabulous idea, and after noisily loading all the shovels and picks into the truck, we set out.

"Do you really think we'll find the elixir?" Jennifer asked. She was in the back seat with Lochlan, and I was in the front, sitting beside Rafe. I wasn't sure who she'd addressed the question to, but it was Rafe who answered after a slight pause.

"I think it's too easy."

That was interesting because I had sort of felt the same way. However, once Sylvia had made a decision, it was easier to follow along than argue with her. Besides, she could be right and all we had to do was dig in the right place to find the witch's secret stash of eternal youth. And, while we were there, we might want to slip inside Karmen's house and have another look around. I was positive that there was something we'd missed. Some clue that would tell us who'd murdered her.

Fortunately, Karmen's property was far from anyone else, so it would be very unlikely that neighbors would alert the police to strange goings-on. Still, we took no chances. We parked on the road leading up to her drive rather than turning into the drive itself. This meant that we had to walk down her private lane. Naturally, the vampires had excellent night vision, so it wasn't like we needed flashlights. My night vision wasn't bad, but it wasn't vampire-accurate. There was a moon, but it was partly covered by clouds. I had an eerie feeling.

Jennifer came up beside me and said, "This place gives me the creeps," and I knew she was feeling it too.

Then we stopped. Rafe had held up his hand. He turned and said softly, "Do you hear that?"

I strained my ears. I have pretty good hearing, but I didn't hear anything. *Wait.* It sounded like gravel shifting.

Sylvia looked at Rafe. "Someone's here before us."

CHAPTER 18

*R*afe said, "Wait here. I'll go first."

Sylvia stepped forward. "I'm coming with you."

He didn't argue, and the two of them crept silently forward.

Sylvia suddenly turned and whispered, "Lucy, you'd better come too."

I started to follow her, and Jennifer said, "Well, I'm not being left here all by myself with a bunch of vampires," and then she came along. In truth, I don't think she cared about being left with the vampires. She didn't want to miss anything.

I could feel Hester's restlessness behind me. I knew that if it had been anyone but Sylvia who told her to stay put, she'd be following us too. But Sylvia did command obedience in Hester, and based on the fact that they were all doing as she told them, I guessed she commanded obedience from all of them.

As we walked between the pub and the cottage, the sound

grew louder. It was like metal scraping on stone. We moved forward, behind the pub and cottage, to where Karmen's land stretched out quite far. The gardens were pretty, and behind them was a structure rising out of the ground, looking ghostly in the moonlight.

Patrick Herrick had said there was a mausoleum on the land. This must be it, though there was no church nearby and no other graves that I could see. The mausoleum looked old, and there were two stone swans on Roman plinths guarding the entrance. Rafe went up two stairs and to a stout wooden door that locked. Except the door was standing open, and as we grew closer, the noise grew more distinct. There was someone in there. When he eased the door open, I caught the gleam of light.

Even though I was not alone and with some powerful creatures, my heart still began to pound.

We walked in. I think that Rafe had motioned to me and Jennifer to stay back, but naturally we pretended we hadn't seen him. I might be nervous, but I wasn't going to miss the excitement.

It was a mausoleum, or had been. I could just make out the shelves, which I was happy to see were empty of bodies, coffins or ashes. It would have been easy to miss the second door because it was set into the wall, but this too was open. And there were stone stairs leading down into who knew what. But from down below, there was light gleaming up.

Rafe went down the stairs first, Sylvia following close behind. We crept down afterwards, me first and then Jennifer bringing up the rear. The stairs were stone and quite smooth, as though they were in frequent use. Not crumbling and falling apart like I would have expected. This must be the crypt, and I sincerely hoped it was as empty as the mausoleum.

The stairs bent around a corner, and as I went around the bend, the light was so bright, it almost blinded me. There were fluorescent lights overhead. I could smell the dampness and dankness of being underground in a stone vault.

Any coffins or bodies that had been interred down here had been removed, and I was looking at an alchemist's laboratory. Even though I'd never seen one before, I immediately recognized what it was. A gas stove sat in the middle, and there were shelves with beakers, mortars and pestles, jars of all kinds of strange-looking ingredients. But more extraordinary was the woman muttering in the corner.

"Where is it? What have you done with it? Must be here."

Even from the back, I recognized her. "Tilda?"

She swung around. Her hair was wild. Her eyes were wild.

She looked at all of us, then her gaze focused in on Sylvia. "Why aren't you dead? You should be dead."

I could feel Sylvia holding her natural fury in check. I didn't know how much time we had till she blew. But I certainly hoped enough time to figure out exactly what was going on here.

I asked, "Why should she be dead?"

"Because I put enough arsenic in that preparation you bought from Karmen to kill an elephant."

The preparation that was meant for me.

She was admitting it? "You killed Karmen. Why?"

She laughed, a strange, brittle laugh. "Look at me. I'm old and frumpy. I have worked for that witch for twelve years, and she never aged a day while I grew lined and wrinkled. I begged her for her secret, but she claimed it was in her skin creams and I must be using them wrong. Did she think I was a fool?"

Too bad Karmen didn't figure out her assistant was crazy.

"Oh, I suspected sorcery. I suspected witchcraft. But it wasn't until *she* came"—and she pointed at Sylvia here —"and I heard them whispering that I finally understood what was going on. She was an alchemist. And she had the secret elixir of life. That's what she was doing. She had made the elixir of life, and she wouldn't share it with me." She made a sound like a shriek. "Did she think I stayed for the paltry wages? I wanted youth. I wanted another chance at the life I'd wasted."

Sylvia's eyes were beginning to flash, and I saw Rafe put a gentle hand on her wrist. He knew me well enough to know that I was pretty good at getting people to talk. I was young and unassuming. And I had a way of sounding like I was genuinely interested. Well, I was genuinely interested. Why on earth would this woman have killed her boss? But I was beginning to see why.

"So she wouldn't share her secret of eternal youth and beauty with you?" I asked.

"All she had for me was a bad wage and her contempt. So after your friend here offered a huge sum for a piece of her philosopher's stone, I knew the source of her youth. All I had to do was find it."

"But I don't understand. Was Karmen's recipe bad? Or did you add the poison?"

"I did it, fool. She was too crafty to let me see where she kept her elixir of life. But she came with that box and, as she always did, got me to do her dirty work. She said to wrap it up nicely and package it and you'd be by to pick it up." Here she pointed at Sylvia.

"When she was out, I went snooping through her house. I went through everything. And then I found her key. The key to her secret laboratory. But the stone wasn't there. The poison was, though. Arsenic. So I added a liberal dose to the powder before I wrapped it up."

"Why didn't you just keep that stone for yourself?" Sylvia asked. I'd been wondering the same thing. It was the logical thing to do.

Her eyes flashed. "Because she'd have known I took it. Besides, I didn't just want enough for myself. What's the point of living forever if you've got no money? I could make a fortune selling youth to others rich enough to pay my price."

Sylvia had settled down now and was calmly listening.

"I knew it was here, you see. I knew her stone had to be here and her recipe to make more. But she grew suspicious of me. I probably asked too many questions. I could feel her watching me all the time. I needed to search her cottage and search the grounds. I had to find the stone and the laboratory that I knew was here, and the recipes."

She banged her fist against the stone wall. "I didn't grow careless. She tricked me. Telling me she was going out, even driving away. I resumed my search, and she caught me in her study, going through her papers. She fired me. Me. After all I'd done for her."

She still seemed stunned that Karmen hadn't wanted to keep employing an assistant who'd paw through her personal papers when she wasn't home.

"I left, pretending to be sorry. I even returned her keys, but I had another set. It was easy enough to let myself into her cottage when she was out and put arsenic in her special tea."

I remembered that special tea that we'd drunk that day. I swallowed hard.

"Then I waited. She always had her special tea every day at three o'clock. So I made sure I was here around that time. Once she was dead, I knew I'd have the place to myself and I could search at my leisure. I carried on working so no one would suspect me. No one knew Karmen had fired me." Now she glared at me and Rafe. "Innocent, hard-working Tilda. Then you two arrived, pushing your way in. Interfering, meddling bride. And you brought the police before I was ready for them."

I didn't have a clue what to say, so kept my mouth shut.

She didn't seem to care. She went on. "But they soon left, after stomping through her house and things with their big boots."

She turned to Rafe, then. "But you did me a favor with your interest in the stencils in the kitchen." She cackled. "Oh, she was a cunning one. The secret was there, on her kitchen walls. Her cellar below the swans. I found her laboratory." She spread her arms and gazed around.

Then her face twisted with fury. "But it's not here. There's nothing here."

"That must be disappointing for you," I said. "I guess she moved everything when she knew you were onto her. I bet you'll never find it."

She screamed then. A scream of rage and frustration that echoed off the dank walls. She reached behind her and picked up what looked to me like an old service revolver. From maybe World War I. Not that I was any expert on guns, but that thing was not new. Where on earth had she found it? Worse, was it loaded? Did she know how to use it?

She waved it around at us.

She looked at Sylvia and with a nasty sneer said, "Well, you wanted to live forever. Try doing it underground."

And then, waving the gun in our general direction, she backed herself up the stairs and flipped off the light.

We were plunged into total darkness. And then I heard the slam of a door and the turning of a key. And then the echo as the second door slammed. There was complete silence for a moment. Both Jennifer and I managed to get our phones out and the flashlight app on at about the same time.

Sylvia said with contempt, "What a ridiculous villain."

Jennifer looked at me, and I looked at her. She said, "How's your door-opening spell?"

I was pleased to say that it was quite good. I'd been practicing.

She said, "After you, then."

I couldn't imagine how terrifying it would have been to be locked down here in normal circumstances, but any one of the four of us could have broken out without any problem at all. I sort of appreciated that Sylvia and Rafe stood back and let us witches handle it. Lighting my way with my phone flashlight, I got to the top of the stairs and found the light switch and turned it on.

I whispered my unlocking spell and had the pleasure of hearing the soft click as the lock released.

Out of courtesy, I let Jennifer use her spell to open the outer door. It wasn't any quicker than mine, but it did the job.

As he came up behind us, Rafe switched out the light.

Sylvia looked quite put out. "Now I suppose we'll have to find her."

Tilda had, of course, run straight into the other vampires. Carlos had hold of her gun, and they were marching her back towards where we'd come from. She was arguing with them that she had no idea what they were talking about, and then she saw us come out of the mausoleum and screamed.

"How did you get out? This is witchcraft. That's what this is. You're monsters!" And then she broke away and began to run. Rafe pushed Carlos's hand down, not that he was in any danger of shooting the woman.

"What shall we do?" I asked, watching the woman run toward the woods at the end of the property.

"One of us will have to take care of her," Sylvia said quite sharply. "We can't have her raving about alchemists and witches and monsters."

"She'll probably just end up sectioned under the Mental Health Act," Lochlan said.

"I don't like it. Too dangerous," Sylvia said.

Rafe looked at me. "Lucy, what do you think?"

"Well, you can't murder the woman. I agree with Lochlan. We're just going to have to hope that no one believes her. If you ask me, she's completely insane anyway."

I could barely see the woman now, still running, still screaming, but then it seemed like she tripped, and we heard a strangled cry.

I ran forward, but of course I was no match for the strength and night vision of vampires. By the time I got to where they were standing, the woman was crumpled on the ground.

"What happened?" Jennifer asked.

Rafe glanced up. "She must have tripped in her haste. She hit her head on a rock."

"Is she...?" I couldn't finish. I felt the darkness of death, and I knew that Jen did too.

"She's dead. Yes."

"Well, that's convenient. But what shall we do with her?" Sylvia asked. "You can't just leave dead women lying all over the ground." Then she seemed to think. "At least, not in these times."

Alfred stepped forward. "I can't think of a better place to put her than in the crypt."

It was a brilliant idea. We'd put her at the bottom of the crypt stairs, leave the doors unlocked, and it would look like an accident. Of course, by the time dawn came, every scrap of alchemist equipment would have been removed, and she'd be found lying in an empty crypt.

Luckily, we had the truck.

Rafe said, "I'll drive Lucy and Jennifer back to town."

"But we can help," I said.

He shook his head firmly. "If anybody comes, we can disappear easily. You'd just be a hindrance." Rude, but true.

He turned to the others. "While I'm gone, get everything out of the crypt and into the truck." He paused for a moment. "And find some supplies for making creams and so on. If there aren't enough in the old pub, find some somewhere and stack them in the crypt so it looks like Tilda was retrieving supplies from the storeroom when she slipped and fell."

"Excellent," Lochlan said. "You get on, and we'll have this done in no time."

To Jennifer and me, he said, "And you two should get a few hours of sleep."

CHAPTER 19

"That's quite the knitting club you have," Jennifer said when we were back at the flat. I put on the kettle, knowing it would be a while before we could sleep. Both of us needed some time to decompress.

"I know. You really got the full-on vampire knitting club experience."

"Do you think they'll be able to put her at the bottom of those stairs so it looks like an accident?"

"Oh yeah."

She thought about it for a second. "I guess they've had some experience trying to make deaths look accidental that really weren't."

I shuddered. I didn't really want to think about that. Instead, I said, "How about some herbal tea?"

"Sure."

While I brewed the tea, she paced up and down my living room. Nyx came downstairs, yawning, to see what was going on. I'd thought she might be out, but I almost got the feeling she'd been waiting for us to come home. Jennifer barely broke stride and bent to pick up the cat and hoist her over her shoulder. There was nothing Nyx enjoyed more. And the two of them paced back and forth. I watched them from my kitchen, filled with affection for the pair of them. I mean, I'd always had a special relationship with Jennifer, but now it seemed like we had something even more special in common.

I brewed a special calming tea for us, knowing that we'd be having a hard time getting to sleep since we were both so wired.

I came out of the kitchen with the two mugs of tea and caught her as she turned from the end of the room and came back towards me. "Smells great," she said, sniffing appreciatively.

"Hopefully it will help us sleep."

"I've been thinking."

Yeah, I'd pretty much got that, since she'd been pacing up and down. I had the same habit. It seemed to help me think too.

She said, "It's great that we figured out who killed that witch, but we definitely need to break the spell on that alchemy book. It was obviously Karmen's."

I'd been thinking, too. I looked at her. "You don't think it would be smarter just to destroy it?"

Shock showed in her face and stopped her in her tracks. "Lucy, she went to a lot of trouble to protect it. I even think she made sure it ended up with Rafe. Didn't you say that it was kind of mysterious that he ended up with the book?"

I nodded. "The people in New Zealand that he supposedly bought it from didn't know anything about it."

She shook a finger at me. "That's witchcraft right there."

I set the two mugs of tea down on the table. "But why would Karmen want Rafe to have her spellbound alchemy book?"

"I don't know that yet. I have a couple of theories. One, he's known to be an expert in that area, and it would be such a curiosity, she'd know that he would keep it. Then she could come back and get it. Because she obviously distrusted her assistant."

I nodded. I sat down on the couch, then I sipped my tea. "That makes sense."

"And my second theory is that she knew that you and Rafe were close. I wonder if she intended for you to have it."

"I think you're reaching there. She wasn't a witch who liked to share her secrets."

"But if she thought she was in danger, she'd want to know that that book would end up in safe hands."

"And you think she saw Rafe's hands, or mine, as a safe haven?"

"Well, they are."

I knew it was true, but I still appreciated the vote of confidence. "That still doesn't mean it's a good idea to hang on to it. She put a strong spell on it for a reason. If that book fell into the wrong hands—" I didn't even want to finish that sentence.

"But to destroy that kind of knowledge seems wrong."

I didn't know what to do. So I sipped more tea. She finally sat down, and Nyx very diplomatically curled up between us, her back end resting against Jennifer's thigh and her head against mine. I stroked her soft fur absently.

Jennifer said, "Before you make any decisions, we need to break that spell."

"You sound pretty confident. Can you do it?" I knew she was a witch, but I didn't know how good she was.

She shook her head. "I could tell right away that I wouldn't be able to break it. Not on my own. You and I together, I suspect, are pretty powerful. But we need a couple more witches. What about your grandmother?"

I shook my head. "Gran's a vampire now. Her witch powers weakened the minute she was turned." I shifted, wishing I could come up with a better idea, but I couldn't. "My cousin Violet is pretty good. And you should probably meet Margaret Twigg anyway. She's the head of our coven. She's very powerful."

Jennifer nodded. "Okay. How's tomorrow night?"

I startled. "You don't waste time, do you?"

She sipped her tea. "I want this whole thing wrapped up before you get married. You want to start with a clean slate, not having old witch business hanging over you."

I totally got what she meant. "Okay."

And so the next night we found ourselves in the middle of the standing stones at midnight. Jennifer, me, Violet, and Margaret Twigg.

"This would be better under a full moon," Margaret said, but I believed our joint magic would be enough to break the spell. At least, I hoped so.

Jennifer insisted that I be the one to carry the book and set it in the center of our circle. I'd never seen her when she was in full-on witch mode, and she was surprisingly take-charge. Margaret Twigg, who was normally the bossy one, seemed a little put out but didn't say anything.

Jen cast the circle and lit the candles with a bit more dramatic flair than I'd seen when she lit them in my flat. I was certain she was showing off for Margaret and Vi.

I could feel a current, almost like electricity, buzzing between us.

Jen raised her hands over the book and said,

"Goddesses of Earth, Fire, Water, and Air, we call on thee
Release the spell from this book so the message is free
Keep its secrets we will
Using it for good not ill
So we will, so mote it be."

At the final words, she brought her hands down toward the book. The electricity I'd felt went pouring out of her fingers, like ten lightning strikes hitting the book. I was afraid it would catch fire, but then the book jumped and flipped open. Streams of colored smoke rose up towards the night sky.

We were all totally silent for a minute, and then Margaret Twigg said, "Well, I'd say that spell's been broken."

Jennifer and I looked at each other. I was almost too scared to go forward and see what the book said, but she was bolder.

"I can't read this book in the candlelight, but it's definitely old. Like, very old."

I came up beside her then and saw exactly what she meant. I'd seen old alchemy texts before. Rafe had quite a few of them, and this looked like those. The pages were faded, the drawings intricate. I reached forward, almost hesitant to touch it, but when my fingers rested on it, I only felt linen paper and calfskin leather binding. I nodded. "The spell is broken."

Margaret looked at both of us. "Your friend has great power," she said. I felt proud, as though I'd had anything to do with Jen's progress as a witch.

"Now, if you'll close the circle, I'll be getting to bed," Margaret said. Compliments were clearly over for the night.

~

THE NEXT DAY we went back to Rafe's place. Olivia, her tools restored, was busy outside with a couple of helpers putting up tents on the grounds. It reminded me how close our wedding was.

Rafe was in his study working. Like me, he was trying to get all his loose ends tied up so that we could actually enjoy a holiday together. When William ushered us into Rafe's study, he looked up, pleased to see me.

"Lucy. Jennifer. Did you get caught up on your sleep?"

Hardly. We'd had another midnight task last night. I felt as jet-lagged as Jen. "Did you get Tilda tidied away?"

"Yes. By the time I returned to Wallingford, nearly everything was done. Theodore had supervised and I believe his time painting sets for a theater company paid off. He staged her body and surroundings so it looked as though she'd fallen on her way to collect supplies for making creams."

"That's great, but how long before anyone finds her body?"

"Oh, that's been done. Seems Karmen's husband arrived yesterday morning and found her. He alerted the police."

"Good." I walked up and put the book in front of him on his worktable.

He opened the cover and nodded. "You've lifted the spell. Well done."

"So far, so good, but it might as well be spellbound for all the sense we can make of it. I need you to translate."

He nodded. Taking his time, he turned each page and looked at it. It wasn't a very big book, and there were a lot of woodcut engravings or whatever you called those things. They featured pictures of suns and moons, snakes wrapped around a person with the face of a woman on one side and a man on the other. I thought that was supposed to be a hermaphrodite. A couple of times he chuckled. Trust Rafe to find an alchemy book funny.

Finally, he said, "A lot of this is what I would call window dressing. I think the pages that are the most interesting are these two."

He read silently and nodded. "What this seems to suggest is that the recipe always needs an existing stone to build on." He glanced up. "Very clever, really. One would need both the recipe and a little of the existing elixir in order to make more."

"You mean like a starter for sourdough bread?" Jen asked.

He chuckled. "Yes. Something like that."

He showed us the page. "And, you see here, the same quotes she had written on her kitchen wall. The cygnet becomes the swan." I pointed to the inked drawings of runes. "And that's the same message on the box, isn't it? As above, so below."

"Yes. Well spotted." I glowed inside with pride.

And then he turned another page and concentrated on it as though he hadn't already read it once. He said, "And this, unless I'm very much mistaken, is her recipe."

"Her recipe? You mean like her formula for her..." I couldn't even say the word.

He finished my sentence. "For the elixir of life. Yes."

And then he picked up the book and handed it to me. He didn't say anything, just handed it to me. But I understood in that moment that he was saying, *This is up to you.*

I was being given a chance to stay young with him, never grow old, without having to be a vampire. It was almost too good to be true.

Jen and I didn't stay long after that. I claimed we had bride stuff to do, but the truth was, Karmen's message had come through.

We waited until we were in the car, driving back towards Oxford, the book clutched in Jennifer's hands. She said, "Tilda was looking in the wrong place."

I nodded. "I think so too."

"But what do we do?"

I sighed. "We have the key now, but Karmen's house is going to be overrun with cops now her death's been discovered."

"You don't think the police will put a guard on the place overnight?"

I shook my head. "Why would they? I don't think they have that kind of staff. And it's not like there's anyone there in danger. Karmen and Tilda are both dead. No, they'll move the body, do some forensic investigation. Between them, I bet the vampires even left a few clues to make it obvious that Tilda killed Karmen. Case closed. If we go in late at night, we'll be okay."

"Maybe we should have a nap so we'll be rested for tonight."

When we got back to my flat, Sylvia and my grand-mother were sitting in my living room, waiting for us. Jennifer jumped. But I was accustomed to these two showing up in my house whenever they felt like it. So much for our nap.

"Sylvia. Gran. What can I do for you? We were just about to act like you two and have a daytime sleep."

Sylvia looked at me sharply. And then her eyes cut to Jennifer, still holding the alchemy book.

"I hear from Margaret Twigg that you were successful in lifting the spell from that book." She didn't end that statement with a lilt, but the question was implied.

There was no point in lying to her. "We did," I said.

She nodded. "And I can tell from the suppressed excitement you two are trying so hopelessly to hide that you've discovered where she keeps her elixir of life."

Jennifer looked at me, but I wasn't going to lie. First of all, Sylvia didn't need it, and second, she'd paid a fortune for me to have that stuff.

I said, "Yes."

She smiled her wintry smile. "Excellent. When shall we go and retrieve it?"

"We're going to go late tonight. But—"

"Don't waste your time on buts, young lady. I paid a lot of money for that elixir. I want to make sure you get it."

AND SO, once again, I found myself traveling the road to Wallingford late at night in the company of my best friend and a much smaller selection of vampires. Theodore was

217

~~driving,~~ and Sylvia and my grandmother sat in the back with us.

Once more, we walked down the driveway in the dead of night. There were signs of recent police activity, and as we grew closer to the mausoleum, I saw police do-not-cross tape. I could feel that the body of Tilda was gone. It was a relief not to feel that heaviness in the pit of the earth beneath us. The two swans seemed almost to be gliding, weightless in the night. We paused in front. The vampires stayed back so as not to interfere with our magic.

Jennifer and I moved closer, and she said, "Will you do the honors?"

She passed me the book and, holding it close to the stone swan on the right of the mausoleum, I read the Latin phrase out loud, as best I could. Then I said, "As above, so below." I was pretty sure I could have said "Open sesame" and it would have worked. The book was the key.

At least I hoped so.

"Come on, Karmen," I said softly. "You know we'll keep your secrets safe."

There was the sound of stone grinding on stone, and the swan's wings seemed to open in front of my eyes. I got out my phone and put that flashlight app on again and played it over the stone swan, and sure enough, there was a cleverly hidden alcove beneath its wing.

Tucked inside was a box exactly like the one I had received as a wedding gift. Just a plain wooden box with runes on the outside. I reached in and picked it up, and then the swan's wing folded in again.

Jennifer said, "Tilda was so close. She had the right idea but not the exact location."

"Also, not the magic, the book or the right intent," I reminded her.

We retraced our steps, and once we were in the Bentley, Sylvia insisted I open the box and make sure that this was the genuine article that she'd paid for this time.

I opened the box and gasped. This wasn't like the other box at all. It was lined in gold.

Sylvia nodded. "Very proper. In alchemy, of course, gold is the purest element."

And there nestling in the gold was another lump of what looked like petrified camel dung. I would get Rafe to test it, of course, but every instinct in my witch's body said that this was the real McCoy. In my hands, I held the secret to eternal youth.

Even if it was the genuine article, would I take it?

I didn't know. And that was okay. I didn't have to decide right away.

When we returned to Oxford, I didn't even take the book up to my flat. I headed to Crosyer Manor. Once there, I bound the book one more time with my own spell, and to be extra safe, I also bound the runic box, and then Rafe put them in the most secure and secret of the several safes he kept in Crosyer Manor.

Once it was fully locked away, he turned to me. "I don't mind, you know," he said, as though answering the question that clamored in my mind. "Whatever you decide."

And that was one of the many reasons why I loved him. I didn't have to explain my hesitation over taking the elixir of life, and he was willing to take me for a mortal term of life if that was my choice. If I decided to remain forever young, that was up to me. All in all, that made him a pretty good groom.

"I will love you forever," I said.

"And I, you." And he kissed me.

As the day of my wedding grew closer, I had fewer and fewer things to worry about. Violet seemed to change her attitude and started taking more responsibility in the shop. Maybe not having me to lean on was bringing out the best in her. I hoped so. She'd told me that she'd take over the staffing, which she'd have to do anyway for the two weeks I was away. And very generously she said if I needed a longer honeymoon, that would be okay. She'd managed the shop when I'd been in New Zealand, after all, and done a fine job. I suspected that going forward, I'd spend less time here, especially if we were franchising so Gran could have a shop of her own in Cornwall.

We picked up the bridesmaid dresses, and the final fitting had me getting misty-eyed again. These three beautiful women that I adored looked stunning in their dresses. We all went out for lunch after the fitting, and I gave them their bracelets.

Naturally, I had imbued each one with a little special magic.

I liked to think that Alice would be wearing a special protection amulet for her and her baby without even knowing it. And when the baby was born, I'd make sure the little one had something special too. The witches, of course, knew what I was up to. But who doesn't need a little extra magic in their lives?

"What will you do, once Lucy's married?" Violet asked Jen. "If you want to stay on in Lucy's flat, I can show you around Oxford. Take you sightseeing."

Jen looked pleased. "Thanks, I'd like that. I thought I might do some traveling while I'm here."

"Come down to Cornwall before you leave," I said. "Promise?"

She looked really pleased to be asked. "I'd love to see Cornwall. I'll definitely come and see you."

My wedding day arrived. After all the times I'd woken up in the night with a pounding heart thinking something would go wrong, nothing did. The sun shone brightly, which wasn't too terrible for the vampires, as everything was under cover.

Margaret Twigg was the officiant, after all. She'd outdone herself for the occasion, wearing a beautiful blue embroidered gown with rows of crystal beads. Her corkscrew hair was as untamed as ever.

My attendants looked beautiful. My dad cleaned up really nicely. His beard was trimmed, his hair was freshly cut, and he was wearing a brand-new suit. We got ready to move forward through a trellis of orange blossoms and up a carpet that led to the veranda where Rafe was waiting.

My dad said, "Are you ready, Lucy?"

I took a breath and felt the truth in my heart. "I've never been readier for anything."

The music changed, and my husband-to-be turned to look at me with my whole future in his eyes.

And I took my first step forward into that future.

∿

~~Thanks for reading~~ *Ribbing and Runes.* I hope you'll consider leaving a review, it really helps.

While you're waiting for the next adventure of the *Vampire Knitting Club*, have you tried the *Vampire Book Club* yet? Here's a peek.

∽

The Vampire Book Club, Chapter 1

HAVE you ever wondered what your life would be like if you'd made one crucial decision differently? What if you hadn't married that man that everyone said was perfect? If you'd taken the job you wanted instead of that one with the good medical benefits? What if you'd moved to New York after college instead of Seattle?

I used to imagine what would have happened if I'd taken the other path. Maybe not the road less traveled, just not traveled by me. It was a harmless exercise to pass the time while I toiled at my boring job, safe from any threat of change.

Until one day I messed with fate.

And I was punished.

I got change all right. More than I could have imagined. My staid life was uprooted. My road was forked. Frankly, I was forked.

At forty-five, I was both divorced and widowed (from the same man), I lost the secure but dull job I'd had for ten years, and the powers that be sent me across the sea to Ireland.

It all happened so fast, my head was still spinning when

my Aer Lingus flight from Seattle landed in Dublin. From there, I took a train to Cork. It was early May, and as I looked out the window, I began to realize why they called Ireland the Emerald Isle. It was so vibrantly green, and between fields of cows and sheep, ruined castles and cottages, we stopped at pretty-sounding towns and cities to let passengers on and off. I smiled when we passed through Limerick and started making up rhymes in my head. They weren't very good, but they passed the time.

There once was a misguided witch
Who tried a man's fate to switch
Her punishment set
To Ireland she must get
But better than feathers and pitch!

From Cork city, I got a bus, though I vowed to come back and explore the pretty city when I was settled. Finally, jet-lagged and travel-weary, I arrived in my new home. The town of Ballydehag.

The bus let me off in front of Finnegan's Grocery. As the curly-haired driver retrieved my two heavy suitcases from the storage compartment underneath the bus, I thanked him. He replied, "Good luck to you, ma'am."

There's a way of wishing a person luck that sounds like you actually wish them good things, and then there's a way of wishing a person good luck that sounds more like, "What on earth have you done?"

I was wondering what on earth I'd done, too, but I was here, now. I pulled my phone out with the address of my new home and then stared vaguely about me. I had no idea where I was, except that this was clearly the main street of a pretty Irish village. The street was lined with shops. A couple of old men in caps sat outside a coffee shop regarding me. I wondered if the arrival of the bus from Cork was a big event. And didn't that say a lot about how exciting this town was?

I couldn't think of anything else to do but go into Finnegan's and hope whoever worked there might know Rose Cottage.

I didn't think my suitcases would even fit through the narrow front door of the shop, and besides, this didn't look like much of a high-crime area, so I pushed my two cases up against the white plaster wall and walked in.

It was like stepping into the past. Narrow rows with shelves of groceries stretched from ceiling to floor and seemed to contain everything from eggs to pest-control products.

I heard voices and turned to the right and the only checkout. A plump woman with curly gray hair stood behind the counter. She wore a green cardigan with the sleeves rolled up her wrists and all the mother-of-pearl buttons done up. The edge of the sweater was scalloped, and the collar of a crisp, white blouse framed her face. She was gossiping with two customers who stood on the opposite side of the counter. "Hello?" I interrupted.

The three stopped talking and all turned to stare at me. I smiled brightly and tried to look nonthreatening. "I'm wondering if you can help me. Do you have the number of a taxi?"

They all looked at each other as though they had never

heard the word taxi before. "A taxicab?" I tried again. "I'm trying to get to a place called Rose Cottage. Do you know where that is?"

The man, tall and thin with pale blue eyes, looked as though a great puzzle had been solved. "Rose Cottage. Ah." He nodded. The other two nodded as well.

There was silence. Me again? "Could you direct me to Rose Cottage? I have two suitcases outside. I was hoping to get a cab to take me there."

The man scratched his head. "I could fetch me wheelbarrow."

The woman behind the counter shook her head at him. "A wheelbarrow. Honestly. I can drive you around, love. It's not far. Danny, you come and stand behind this counter, and if anyone wants to buy anything, you just write down what it is, or they can wait until I get back. I won't be a minute."

Was this woman actually going to leave her post to drive a complete stranger? "I don't want to take you away from your work," I stammered.

"Oh, it's no trouble. And you've chosen a good time. We're not very busy."

Danny looked quite pleased to walk behind the counter and stand there very importantly. He began tidying up open packs of chocolate bars as though he owned the place.

"I'm Kathleen McGinnis," said the woman who'd come from behind the cash desk. I warmed to her immediately, but I'd warm to anyone who was willing to drive me to my new home. "And you must be Quinn Callahan."

I did a double take. "You knew I was coming?"

"I've been on the lookout for you."

Read the rest of the *Vampire Book Club* or sign up for my newsletter at NancyWarrenAuthor.com to hear about all of my new releases.

A Note from Nancy

Dear Reader,

Thank you for reading the Vampire Knitting Club series. I am so grateful for all the enthusiasm this series has received. I have plenty more stories about Lucy and her undead knitters planned for the future.

I hope you'll consider leaving a review and please tell your friends who like cozy mysteries.

Review on Amazon, Goodreads or BookBub.

Your support is the wool that helps me knit up these yarns.

Join my newsletter for a free prequel, *Tangles and Treasons*, the exciting tale of how the gorgeous Rafe Crosyer was turned into a vampire.

I hope to see you in my private Facebook Group. It's a lot of fun. www.facebook.com/groups/NancyWarrenKnitwits

Until next time,
Happy Reading,

Nancy

Cat's Paws and Curses - A Holiday Whodunnit

Vampire Knitting Club Boxed Set: Books 1-3

Vampire Knitting Club Boxed Set: Books 4-6

Vampire Knitting Club Boxed Set: Books 7-9

Village Flower Shop: Paranormal Cozy Mystery

Peony Dreadful - Book 1

The Great Witches Baking Show: Culinary Cozy Mystery

The Great Witches Baking Show - Book 1

Baker's Coven - Book 2

A Rolling Scone - Book 3

A Bundt Instrument - Book 4

Blood, Sweat and Tiers - Book 5

Crumbs and Misdemeanors - Book 6

A Cream of Passion - Book 7

Cakes and Pains - Book 8

Whisk and Reward - Book 9

Gingerdead House - A Holiday Whodunnit

The Great Witches Baking Show Boxed Set: Books 1-3

Vampire Book Club: Paranormal Women's Fiction Cozy Mystery

Crossing the Lines - Prequel

The Vampire Book Club - Book 1

Chapter and Curse - Book 2

A Spelling Mistake - Book 3

A Poisonous Review - Book 4

Toni Diamond Mysteries

Toni is a successful saleswoman for Lady Bianca Cosmetics in this series of humorous cozy mysteries.

Frosted Shadow - Book 1

Ultimate Concealer - Book 2

Midnight Shimmer - Book 3

A Diamond Choker For Christmas - A Holiday Whodunnit

Toni Diamond Mysteries Boxed Set: Books 1-4

The Almost Wives Club

An enchanted wedding dress is a matchmaker in this series of romantic comedies where five runaway brides find out who the best men really are!

The Almost Wives Club: Kate - Book 1

Secondhand Bride - Book 2

Bridesmaid for Hire - Book 3

The Wedding Flight - Book 4

If the Dress Fits - Book 5

The Almost Wives Club Boxed Set: Books 1-5

Take a Chance series

Meet the Chance family, a cobbled together family of eleven kids who are all grown up and finding their ways in life and love.

Chance Encounter - Prequel

Kiss a Girl in the Rain - Book 1

Iris in Bloom - Book 2

Blueprint for a Kiss - Book 3

Every Rose - Book 4

Love to Go - Book 5

The Sheriff's Sweet Surrender - Book 6

The Daisy Game - Book 7

Take a Chance Boxed Set: Prequel and Books 1-3

Abigail Dixon Mysteries: 1920s Cozy Historical Mystery

In 1920s Paris everything is très chic, except murder.

Death of a Flapper - Book 1

For a complete list of books, check out Nancy's website at
NancyWarrenAuthor.com

ABOUT THE AUTHOR

Nancy Warren is the USA Today Bestselling author of more than 100 novels. She's originally from Vancouver, Canada, though she tends to wander and has lived in England, Italy and California at various times. While living in Oxford she dreamed up The Vampire Knitting Club. Favorite moments include being the answer to a crossword puzzle clue in Canada's National Post newspaper, being featured on the front page of the New York Times when her book Speed Dating launched Harlequin's NASCAR series, and being nominated three times for Romance Writers of America's RITA award. She has an MA in Creative Writing from Bath Spa University. She's an avid hiker, loves chocolate and most of all, loves to hear from readers!

The best way to stay in touch is to sign up for Nancy's newsletter at NancyWarrenAuthor.com or www.facebook.com/groups/NancyWarrenKnitwits

To learn more about Nancy and her books
NancyWarrenAuthor.com

facebook.com/AuthorNancyWarren

twitter.com/nancywarren1

instagram.com/nancywarrenauthor

amazon.com/Nancy-Warren/e/B001H6NM5Q

goodreads.com/nancywarren

bookbub.com/authors/nancy-warren

Made in the USA
Las Vegas, NV
24 June 2022

50653739R00134